Mermaids & Mood Swings

Harrow Bay, Volume 7

Aurelia Skye

Published by Amourisa Press, 2022.

Blurb

When Jody's BFF blows through town, she has to shield Daphne from the truth of Harrow Bay. Her friend complicates that when she starts dating Ryland. Jody is nervous about her being with a vampire, especially when Daphne doesn't know what he is. With Drake busy chasing an extremely dangerous, high-level escapee from Hell, and having to contend with the temporary deputy sent to fill in for Michael while he's on vacation, Jody feels stretched thin.

Willa and Patty traverse new ground, and Isabel makes a new friend. Things are much the same, but everything is different and constantly in flux. In other words, it's a normal day in Harrow Bay...as normal as things ever are. Jody just has to keep it all together, hide the secret of the town, and potentially protect her friend from a suitor who might want to give more than love bites. No problem. Right?

Chapter One

Jody

"I'm so glad you could spend tonight with me," said Jody as she cuddled against Drake. She spoke softly to him not to disturb her mother and grandmother, who were both engrossed in the movie they were watching. It was Friday night, the day after Thanksgiving, and the end of Jody's vacation.

She doubted much would happen over the weekend, but she was technically back on duty as of Saturday morning. Unfortunately for Drake, he had been on duty for the last several days in pursuit of an escaped demon. She was lucky to see him for a couple of hours yesterday on Thanksgiving and even luckier when he had managed to get away for a while tonight. "I'm worried Luc is running you ragged."

He shrugged against her. "It's definitely not a personal thing. He has most of his bounty hunters on alert for Honsiu."

She nodded, aware of the situation and a little tense about the idea of a high-level demon having escaped Hell. If she understood it correctly, coming and going was one of those privileges one earned or had conferred upon them. A demon couldn't simply stroll out from Hell, and their boss tended to take it personally when they left without permission.

"Let's not think about it tonight. I'd much rather hold you and watch this engrossing movie."

Jody tilted her head and slanted a glance at him, not bothering to hide her skepticism. "Yeah, I'm sure you're terribly vested in what happens to these old Southern ladies."

He chuckled. "I do have a soft spot for old ladies." He pinched her on the butt.

She let out a squeal of surprise before pulling away from him. "Jerk." Her tone was full of affection though.

He laughed. "I'm just kidding. You're certainly not old."

Jody winced slightly as she shifted, realizing there was a pain in her lower back from the way she had been lying against Drake. "Let's just say, I'm not young either."

"It suits me just fine. I like you just the way you are." He took her hand, and his manner was so gentle that it was difficult to believe he wasn't telling her the truth.

For some stupid reason, the back of her eyes burned, and she blinked rapidly.

"I think someone's here," said Willa.

Jody started to ask her why she thought that, but the doorbell rang a second later. Apparently, Willa hadn't lost her sharp sense of hearing even after she'd started to age. When no one else made any effort to move, she said, "I'll get it."

She stood up, easing past Drake to move to the front door as the bell rang again. Whomever waited was clearly impatient, and she bit back the urge to reprimand them for repeatedly ringing the doorbell as she opened it a second later.

"Hello, Sheriff," said Daphne Valentine as she blew in through the door, enveloping Jody in a tight hug.

Jody hugged back instinctively, with a gasp of surprise on her lips as she embraced her best friend. She hadn't seen Daphne for more than a year, but it immediately felt like they hadn't been apart at all. When the hug ended, she pulled back slightly. "I had no idea you were in the area."

"I was in Portland." She dropped her voice to a pseudo whisper. "They have an amazing stem cell program there for wrinkles." She touched her barely lined face in a self-conscious fashion. "I knew you were kind of in the area, though you'd moved away from your old place. I called your mom to surprise you, and she told me how to find Harrow Bay."

Jody glanced at her mom, who was smiling, realizing there might've been more to her mother's detection of Daphne's arrival than good hearing. "This is a fabulous surprise." She put her arm around Daphne's waist and pulled her into the living room, giving her friend a moment to greet Isabel and Willa before she turned her to Drake. "Drake, this is my best friend, Daphne. Daphne, meet Drake."

Daphne looked intrigued. "So, this is Drake?"

Drake arched a brow. "You've heard of me?"

"Some good and some bad," said Daphne in a neutral tone. She took the other seat beside him, staring at him for a moment. "I know Jody likes you. It predisposes me to liking you too, unless of course you hurt my friend. If you do, you probably won't like what happens next."

Drake shifted uneasily, and Jody chuckled as she sat down beside him. "She's mostly bark, no bite."

Daphne still looked serious. "I can make an exception." Her tone was menacing for a moment, but then her expression lightened. "Of course, if you know what's good for you, I won't have to."

Jody shook her head. "You don't have to try to intimidate him."

"Oh, I didn't mean it that way. I meant, if he's smart, he'll hold on to you. He must be something special to have caught your attention, so I'm assuming he has more than his fair share of brains." Daphne looked him up and down again, making Drake visibly squirmed. "He certainly got his share of height, didn't he?"

"And muscles," said Jody, unable to deny she was enjoying a little bit of Drake's discomfort at the way her friend was so frankly assessing him. Of course, she couldn't imagine he truly felt intimidated, since he was half-demon. He could easily subdue Daphne if she ever felt the inclination to go after him as she'd threatened, but he still seemed ill-at-ease.

She put a hand on his thigh, squeezing lightly, and he seemed to relax. She leaned past him to look at Daphne. "Besides the stem cell thing, what are you doing in the area? Last I heard, you were in Milan."

Daphne pulled a face. "Things didn't work out with Esteban." She shrugged a shoulder.

Jody winced in sympathy. "I guess he wasn't going to be husband number five?"

"Jody, shame on you for bringing that up," said Willa with a starched look.

Jody and Daphne laughed together. "It's all right, Willa," said Daphne. "It's hardly a secret that I've been married four times, is it?"

Drake cleared his throat. "I didn't know that."

Daphne shrugged. "Everyone else did. I just have bad luck with men."

"No, you have bad taste in men. There's a big difference," said Jody with a hint of teasing.

Willa shook her head. "The things you say to your friend."

"It's because we're such good friends that I can say that, Mom." Jody looked at Daphne again, swearing her friend was exactly the same. Her skin was nicely tanned, though that was probably from a product, since Daphne didn't want to risk too many sunspots by allowing herself much sun exposure.

Her dark hair was thick and glossy, with nary a strand of silver or gray appearing, either naturally or perhaps with the assistance of a skilled hairdresser. Her brows were perfectly plucked, and her makeup was expertly applied even though it was late in the evening, and she had probably been traveling for at least part of the day.

She was as glamorous and beautiful as ever, but she still seemed to have that same restless edge about her, the one that made Jody worry about her and think Daphne might never find exactly what she was looking for. "You're staying with us, aren't you?"

"Of course. Willa volunteered to bunk with Isabel so I could have her room."

"Isabel didn't volunteer for that," said Gram in a grumpy tone. "I'm not sleeping with Willa. She snores."

"Hardly, Mother. You're the one who snores. I'm the one making the sacrifice here."

Gram glared at her daughter. "You're not making a sacrifice, because I'm not sleeping with you. Daphne can have my room, and I'll take the couch."

Daphne frowned. "I'm not going to do that to you, Isabel. A woman your age needs her bed."

"Don't tell me about my age, missy." Isabel wagged a finger at Daphne. "I know exactly what I can handle. Just a couple weeks ago..." She trailed off, clearly thinking better of mentioning the events that had happened with Sally Gilling.

Jody was happy to turn the subject away from that as well, since Daphne had no clue about the existence of magic, paranormal things, and the secrets of Harrow Bay. She cleared her throat. "You can just bunk with me."

Daphne grinned. "I figured you'd say that." She looked at Drake. "Would you mind putting those muscles to use by bringing in my luggage?"

As Drake started to stand up, Jody patted his hand. "Be careful. She never packs lightly."

Drake grinned, looking confident. "I'm sure I can handle it."

Jody spent the next few minutes catching up with Daphne as Drake took her friend's keys so he could retrieve her luggage from the rental car. She couldn't help grinning when he returned a few moments later, laden with baggage, including a trunk he carried across his back. Even for Drake's impressive muscles, it seemed like quite a load, and she bit her lip so she didn't giggle. "Would you like some help?"

He huffed at her as he stood at the bottom of the stairs. "I can handle it." With a deep breath, he plowed up the stairs.

Jody watched him go, admiring his tenacity and the way his muscles flexed. It was only when Daphne laughed that she realized her gaze had remained on him, focused squarely on his butt, and she blushed as she looked back at her friend.

"You really are smitten with him. I know you've talked a lot about him but seeing you actually so into a guy is a little foreign to me, I admit."

Jody was a bit self-conscious, but she struggled to hide it. "What can I say? He's different than any man I've ever met." In so many ways, and she felt bad for a moment that she couldn't explain it all to Daphne. She couldn't risk the secrets of the town even with her best friend though. Of course, Daphne would forget anything she learned within a few weeks of leaving Harrow Bay, but it was better to shield her from the truth if possible.

"If he makes you happy, that's all that matters." Daphne moved closer, bridging the distance between them, and hugged her again. "It's so good to see you. I can't believe it's been more than a year."

"Time flies when you're looking for husband number five," said Jody as she laughed.

"What can I say? I like being in love."

"The alimony checks don't hurt either." Jody winked at her.

Willa was tutting under her breath, clearly disapproving of their exchange, but she didn't reprimand Jody this time. Instead, she just muttered something to herself before getting up. "I think I'll go to bed. It was lovely to make the surprise happen with you, Daphne." Willa moved closer, bending down and pressing a kiss to Daphne's forehead. "I'll see you tomorrow, and we can catch up then about all the pleasant things in your life."

"Which means you don't want to hear about my four ex-husbands or my three stepkids, right, Willa?" Daphne winked at her.

Willa flushed and looked away. "Good night."

Gram stood up a moment later, coming closer as well. "Willa isn't one for dealing with the harsh realities." She shrugged. "If it works for her, what's the problem, right?" She leaned down slightly and hugged Daphne, who started to get to her feet. "No, don't get up. I'll spend time with you tomorrow as well. Jody's technically back on duty, though hopefully she won't be called in with you visiting."

After wishing them good night, Isabel disappeared up the stairs as Drake came down them.

"I see he knows right where your room is." Daphne winked.

Jody shrugged. "It's a small house." She wasn't about to reveal they had been lovers briefly before taking a time-out after the love spell had worn off. It wasn't that she cared to share that information with Daphne, but she couldn't figure out how to explain it all in a way her friend could understand without mentioning magic.

She sighed softly, realizing this new aspect of her life was going to be harder to deal with than she'd thought, at least when it came to her best friend. Maybe she should just tell her the truth, but she wasn't certain that was a good idea either.

Jody decided to play it by ear and enjoy the time she had with Daphne as they spent the next couple of hours catching up after Drake excused himself too. Jody had tried to get him to stay, but he'd insisted he had to get back to work, and he probably wasn't exaggerating. When he was tracking a demon, there was no such thing as off-hours or time for sleep. Not that she thought he had an active to lead on Honsiu at the moment.

As it got later, Jody couldn't stifle a yawn. "I guess I should get to sleep. There's a chance I might have to work tomorrow. I'm technically on duty, and one of my deputies goes on vacation, so I can't call in sick or anything."

"You're always so responsible." Daphne made it sound almost like a failing, but she softened the criticism with a light hug around Jody's shoulders as they stood up. "I could go to sleep too. It's been a long day. Are sure you don't mind me in your room? I could still sleep on the couch."

Jody shook her head. "It doesn't fold out. You'd be uncomfortable, and it certainly wouldn't be our first slumber party."

"Definitely not. We must have been in kindergarten the first time I slept over, right?"

Jody nodded. "I think it was within a few weeks of meeting each other, so it had to be kindergarten."

"Who would've imagined we'd still be friends almost forty years later?" Daphne looked stricken for a moment. "Not that I'll admit that to anyone else but you."

"You're almost forty-three, not eighty-three. What's the big deal?" As she led Daphne upstairs, she couldn't help thinking of her grandmother, who was full of energy and a real pistol. "I think eighty-three isn't necessarily all that bad either, at least if you age as well as Gram has."

"I prefer not to age at all." Daphne stepped through the door Jody held open for her, so she'd know which room to enter. Her friend looked around for a moment, nodding. "This is nice. It's very much your style, which is kind of utilitarian with a little bit of decoration among your functionality."

"I'm sorry it's not Queen Anne-style."

Daphne shrugged. "Nothing is ever perfect." She sighed. "I should know after the number of relationships I've tried out."

Jody didn't tease her about it, knowing despite Daphne's apparent lack of care for the topic, she truly was somewhat distraught that she'd never found the perfect fit. At least Daphne valued herself enough not to stay in relationships that were going nowhere, and that was one thing Jody had always admired about her.

She supposed some might chastise Daphne for not sticking with her relationships, that they might look down on her for having four failed marriages, but Jody had always seen it as proof that Daphne knew her own worth and the value of her time. It didn't hurt either that Jody had only liked one of the four exes, since she hadn't felt any of the other three had truly respected how special Daphne was.

She let Daphne have the bathroom first, taking a moment to change into pajamas before sliding into bed. When Daphne left the bathroom a few minutes later, she joined Jody and pulled back the covers. When she started to get into bed, Jody saw some faint lines on her leg. "Are you all right?"

Daphne hastily covered her legs from view. "I'm fine. It just a few varicose veins." She was clearly self-conscious about it as she lowered her voice to whisper, "That was another reason I was in Portland. They have a fantastic vein specialist there. She is world-renowned."

"Are they dangerous? I mean, are they going to increase your risk of a heart attack or something?"

Daphne shook her head. "They just make it look awful if I wear a bikini or a dress."

"At least it's nothing life-threatening then." She leaned over, reaching for the lamp. "Is it okay if I turn off the light?"

"Sure. We can talk in the dark, and I'm sure we'll be up half the night doing just that."

Jody laughed, certain her friend was correct. It was always like that with them, no matter how brief or long the separation of time between visits. She turned off the light, and as Daphne predicted, they spent the next couple of hours talking about nothing important, but it was still satisfying. Daphne was still talking as Jody fell asleep.

***

Jody only had to work a little bit that day, sent only on two calls and otherwise staying at home, so she was well-rested and energized when Daphne suggested they go out for the evening. There weren't a lot of dinner or entertainment options, but they had dinner at the steakhouse before going to *Shoot and Shots,* where Randy Carlson greeted Jody with a familiar nod. Jody introduced Daphne, and they took a table in the corner. "You haven't mentioned it."

Daphne stiffened slightly. "Mentioned what?" Randy arrived then with their first round of shots, and Daphne downed one before ordering another.

"What day it is." Jody had been careful not to mention it either, waiting for Daphne to broach the subject, but her friend still hadn't.

Daphne grimaced. "I prefer not to think about it."

"It's your birthday. We can't let it go uncelebrated."

"What's there to celebrate? I'm forty-three. End of story." She finished her second shot and seemed to be looking for Randy. "You know how I feel about birthdays."

"You don't have to love them, but it's probably not healthy to let them go by unacknowledged."

Daphne shrugged. "Acknowledging them gives them power."

Jody chuckled softly, imagining those words applied to any number of situations, at least in Harrow Bay. "A philosophy my mother can embrace. Anyway, happy birthday." As she said that, she lifted her shot of bourbon and swallowed as Randy returned.

He beamed. "We have a birthday girl here?"

"Reluctantly." Daphne looked at the shot Randy had brought before frowning. "Maybe you should just bring the bottle."

Randy nodded, returning to the bar. He was back within seconds, setting the bottle between them. When he departed again, Daphne poured herself another and took it quickly.

"Ease up there. I'd hate to have to arrest you for being drunk and disorderly," said Jody with a hint of teasing, though she couldn't help being a little concerned about Daphne's prodigious consumption. It wasn't like her friend.

"I promise you won't have to arrest me. I can stumble out under my own power." Daphne swallowed another shot, but at least she didn't refill her glass this time.

"Seriously, is there something wrong?" Jody set aside her empty glass as she leaned closer, bridging the distance between them.

Daphne nibbled on her lower lip for a minute. "I don't know. This birthday just seems worse than the one before, and the one before that was bad enough. I thought forty was going to kill me, and I just keep getting closer and closer to fifty."

"I kind of get it. I mean, I'm the same age, but I guess I'm not as worried about it."

"Why would you be? You have a career and your family, and you might even have proper romantic prospects with Drake. He seems like a nice guy, and you deserve that. What do I have?"

"A fabulous fashion sense, gorgeous face and body, and high intelligence. And a trust fund."

Daphne looked like she might reject that after a moment, but then she slowly smiled. "Those are things to celebrate." She refilled their glasses again. "To all the fabulous things we have."

Jody lifted her shot glass and clinked it against Daphne's before swallowing the alcohol and setting down her glass again. She winced at the burning sensation as the bourbon worked its way down her throat. Shots were never her favorite, but she didn't mind having them occasionally.

As she turned her head slightly, she saw a familiar face. Jody couldn't keep from wincing slightly as the hairs on the back of her neck rose. Ryland Santiri was across the bar, and she couldn't help speculating that the people with him were also vampires.

Daphne seemed to follow her gaze, and her eyes brightened. "Who's he?"

"Just a local." Jody kept her tone brusque and deliberately looked away from Ryland. She didn't want to have to explain to Daphne why she was uneasy around him. He gave every appearance of having his vampire coven together and keeping them all on the straight-and-narrow, but there was still the caveman instinct in her that responded to being around a predator like Ryland. It urged her to run away and hide, which she couldn't do. As the sheriff of Harrow Bay, she didn't have that luxury even if she wanted to.

Not that Ryland had done anything to make her want to run away from him, or to suspect that he would. Other than that one incident shortly after she'd arrived, when he had to put down the feral vampire, she hadn't really had any interaction with him. It was just a general sense of unease, and she supposed perhaps it was prejudice on her part that inspired it. Just because he was a vampire didn't make him a bad person.

They spent the next couple of hours talking and shooting pool while Daphne steadily consumed a good part of the bottle Randy had brought. When he returned with new glasses, Jody indicated he should take the bottle that time. Daphne let out a laughing protest, but she was barely sitting upright in her chair. She certainly didn't have the ability to express her objection to him whisking away the alcohol.

"We should probably get you home," said Jody. "You might have a headache tomorrow."

"I'll just have Isabel do a little magic for me."

Jody stiffened. "I... What?"

"Don't you remember your Gram's magical hangover concoction? You feel better within a half-hour of drinking it."

It took Jody a moment to remember, but she slowly nodded. "Yeah, I guess we used that more than once during our college years." Her heart returned to its normal rate when she realized Daphne hadn't actually been referencing magic.

Of course, her friend had no way of knowing that Isabel was trying to learn magic and develop what meager skills she had. She hadn't been referring to true magic or some kind of hangover potion. Daphne had just been speaking in general terms, but Jody's outlook had shifted over the last few months, and it was difficult not to read more into such references.

"I'm not sure I want to leave yet." As she spoke, Daphne stood up. She swayed for a moment, and Jody was afraid she might have to hold her up. Somehow, Daphne maintained her balance as she started walking across the room. Jody frowned, uncertain if she should go after her.

When Daphne paused in front of the table where Ryland sat, Jody was tense. She wasn't certain what they said, since it was too far away, but a couple of minutes later, they were dancing in front of the jukebox. They were the only ones dancing, but it didn't seem to bother either Daphne or Ryland, and Jody tried not to worry about her friend's interest in the vampire.

Daphne often had quick and fleeting attractions. It didn't mean her friend was in danger, or that Jody had to warn her that the latest love interest was a bloodsucking vampire. That it was cows' blood instead of human blood didn't necessarily make it a whole lot better.

At the end of the song, Jody was reluctantly impressed at the way Ryland put his arm around Daphne and brought her back to the table, seating her carefully. He nodded to Jody before returning to his table.

"He's nice," said Daphne in a dreamy voice. "Seems a little old-world or something though. I've never dated a man with such exquisite manners before. He seemed practically chivalrous."

It probably had something to do with the fact he'd maybe been alive during the age of chivalry, but Jody managed not to make that comment. "Do you think we should go now?"

Daphne sighed. "Fine, Mom." She was obviously a little irritated at Jody's mother-henning, but she stood up. It was with such a dramatic flounce that she almost fell.

Jody rushed forward and held her up, staring at her friend. "Are you able to walk?"

"I'm just fine." Daphne hiccupped then, and she swayed. "You might need to give me a hand." She giggled as she collapsed against Jody.

Jody had no objection to helping her but helping was a little bit different than dragging half of Daphne's weight, since her friend was pretty out of it. It seemed like the alcohol had hit her in the last few minutes, and Jody was wondering how she was going to get her to the car short of doing something like casting a spell to carry her when Ryland appeared.

"Do you need some help?"

Despite her reservations, Jody nodded. "I think Daphne had a little too much to drink."

"Let me help you then."

Jody had expected him to put his arm around Daphne's waist to balance her, but instead, he picked up her friend like she weighed nothing and started walking out of the bar. Jody grabbed her purse and Daphne's as well and followed behind him after leaving a stack of bills on the table.

When she came out of the bar, Ryland already had Daphne at the SUV, and Jody quickly unlocked it for him. As he started to lift her friend inside after Jody opened the door, Daphne snuggled closer, put her arm around his neck, and kissed Ryland right on the mouth.

It wasn't a gentle or tame kiss either. There was enough passion to make Jody blush lightly and look away, though she'd seen plenty of public displays of affection before, most notably during the effects of the love spell.

Ryland pulled away first, clearing his throat. He appeared to be flushing, and she wondered how a vampire did that, unless he'd fed recently. The idea was unsettling, so she tried not to think about it as he lifted Daphne and put her in the SUV, fastening her seatbelt. She waved at him with three of her fingers, and he waved back lamely before closing the door and turning to Jody. "Can you get her out when you get home?"

Jody nodded, certain she'd think of something. If Daphne was that out of it, her friend was unlikely to notice if she used a little magical assistance to get her inside. "Thanks for your help."

"It was my pleasure." His thoughts seemed to wander for a moment, clearly back to Daphne, as he glanced at her through the window. "Well, good night, Sheriff Shaw."

She nodded at him and watched him walk back into Randy's bar before going around the SUV to get inside. She started to talk to Daphne, but she realized her friend had passed out. Her head was tipped back, and she was snoring loudly.

Jody was unable to resist the urge to pull out her phone to take a picture for posterity, and perhaps to tease Daphne a bit about it in the future. Part of her contemplated the idea of showing Daphne to demonstrate just how out of control she had let herself get, but she decided she was being too heavy-handed, since the other woman didn't make this kind of thing a habit.

As Jody drove home, she tried not to be too concerned about her friend. She doubted Daphne had developed a drinking problem in the year or so they hadn't seen each other. No doubt, it was just the fact she had turned forty-three today, and she knew Daphne had been struggling with aging. Hopefully, Daphne would be over it by tomorrow and feel much better, at least after Gram whipped up one of her miracle hangover cures.

This time, Gram might actually be able to infuse it with some real magic, and that would leave Daphne feeling one hundred percent refreshed. Maybe Jody should have Gram temper that effect, but she couldn't imagine letting her friend suffer just so she could learn a lesson that she'd probably already learned many years ago. She couldn't fault Daphne for having a little lapse in control. Birthdays were hard even for Jody, and she wasn't quite as concerned about aging.

She pushed aside her worry, not wanting to overreact, and when they reached her place a short time later, she used a little magic to help carry Daphne inside. Her friend never really woke up and never realized she'd used any magic at all. Instead, she snored lightly as Jody tucked her in, blissfully unaware of the magic surrounding her.

Chapter Two

Isabel

She had steered clear of the Senior Center since the Sally Incident, but curiosity and sheer boredom drove her back that afternoon. She hesitated a long moment before entering. As Kay came to greet her, she braced herself for a cool reception. After all, Kay had been one of Sally's most fervent minions.

Kay gave her a blinding smile. "Hello, Isabel. It's a lovely day, isn't it? We're scrapbooking if you'd like to join us."

She frowned, a little taken aback by the friendliness. "Don't I need something to scrapbook?"

Kay blinked. "Like photos?"

She nodded.

The director waved a hand. "Don't worry about that. You can fill in pages with handwritten memories and fun images."

"That sounds delightfully impersonal." Isabel rolled her eyes as Kay turned back to the main room, but she followed the younger woman. After all, her curiosity hadn't been sated yet.

She entered hesitantly, but there was barely a stir at her presence. She eyed Gil, who'd recently had a hip replacement and had tried to hold Isabel captive at Sally's command, but he didn't seem to remember that. When he caught her looking, he just lifted a hand in a friendly wave.

She took a seat at the table, eyeing the cheerful paper, stickers, myriad generic images of happy places, people, and things, and reached for a set of scissors. She picked them up and started randomly cutting a pastel polka dot page. She was going to have to ask about the situation if she wanted resolution, and it required treading delicately. "So, pretty crazy about Sally, huh?"

A few people stiffened, but most appeared oblivious. Kay blinked. "I'm sorry?"

"Sally and the...incident." Isabel frowned at her.

Kay blinked again. "Sally...Gilling?" Her brow scrunched. "I believe she came here sometimes, but I haven't seen her in a long time."

"At least weeks," said Isabel as she cut the page in an abstract design.

"No, probably not for years." Kay shrugged. "I don't know her well. Are you friends with her? Is she ill?"

"I've noticed she hasn't been at her place at the retirement village," said Gil. "In fact, a new man moved in just a couple days ago."

"Huh." Isabel's response wasn't because someone had taken over Sally's apartment. It was because these people seemed to have only a vague recollection of her. She couldn't help wondering if it was willful self-deception, the magic of the town working on their memories, or perhaps an aftereffect of Sally's spell.

"You'll have to tell us what you like to do," said Kay in a warm fashion as she pasted a picture of a baby frolicking with a dog on a yellow-striped page. She seemed to be doing it mindlessly.

That was hardly surprising. The woman was mindless. Isabel kept the unkind thought to herself. "I'm not sure why you'd care." She could admit she still smarted from the way they'd all shunned her at Sally's behest.

If Kay thought her tone or words were odd, she showed no sign. "We like to have activities all our members enjoy. What do you like?"

"Drinking wine and spicy foods." She thought about mentioning learning magic but held back.

Kay blinked. "Oh...I...I'm not sure you'll find many others with that interest." She frowned but then brightened. "I bet we could get a member of the university annex to come talk to us about growing grapes though. I know for a fact they'll grow here, since I have a lovely wild bush in my back yard. I didn't even know what it was when Davis and I bought the place, but it keeps coming back year after year. The grapes are sweet and delicious."

"You have to grow a different variety for wine." Not that Isabel cared about learning how to grow grapes, but she couldn't help riling Kay and enjoying it. The woman's forehead wrinkled each time she faced a curveball.

"Oh." She seemed unenthusiastic for a moment before brightening. "You must know all about it. Why don't you tell us more?"

Isabel shrugged. "I don't really." She set down the scissors, finding the place claustrophobic. Even without Sally's presence, there was a definite *Stepford Wives* vibe to the place that still left her uneasy. She pushed back from her seat. "Thanks for the scrapbooking lesson, but I have to go."

Kay looked disappointed. "If you leave your number, I'll call you when I set up a visit from the annex."

"Yeah, sure." She didn't seem to detect Isabel's lack of interest as she went back to generic scrapbooking and offering an occasional comment on the conversations happening around her.

Isabel shook her head as she exited the room. She couldn't help wondering if they were all normally sheep, or if there was a residual effect of Sally's magic acting upon them.

She was heading toward the exit when a wheelchair plowed into her left knee, making Isabel wince and curse. "Watch where you're..." She trailed off as she looked down at the woman in the chair. She was diminutive and clearly a few grapes short of a picnic. She gave Isabel a vacant stare as drool trailed down her chin.

Isabel looked around, certain the woman wasn't there alone. "Hello? Is someone with...her?"

After a moment, the sound of footsteps reached her just before a large woman rounded the corner. She was around Isabel's age, with a giant red hat that obscured half her face, and an impressive array of flowers and feathers sticking up from it. Isabel was mesmerized by the way it swayed as the woman hurried toward them. Hurrying be a subjective term at their age.

"Mother, there you are." She sounded exasperated, but in a gentle way, and her hand was light as she deftly wiped her mother's chin with a tissue. She looked at Isabel then. "Thank you for finding my mother."

Isabel rubbed her knee without thought. "It was more like she found me."

The woman flushed. "It's my fault." She confided that in a whisper. "I don't think I put on the brake well enough when I popped into the ladies' room."

"It's fine. She maybe shouldn't be alone though."

"Once, Billy put a toad in the pocket of my best school dress. Mama whipped him good," said the older woman with a pleased chuckle.

"Yes, I remember." Her daughter didn't sound impatient, but she'd clearly heard the story before. She looked around for a moment. "Shall we sit and get some coffee?"

Isabel wanted to escape the Senior Center, but there was a desperate edge about the daughter that gave her pause. "Um, sure." She gestured them toward a couch nearby. "How do you take yours?"

"Cream and two sugars." The woman patted her mother's hand. "None for Mother, of course."

Isabel nodded, fetching coffee for both of them, though she had no real interest in the brew. She took a seat near the woman on the couch, surreptitiously ensuring the brakes were on Houdini's wheelchair as she did so.

"Thank you again for finding Mother." The woman removed her hat to reveal a nearly bald head with only a few black strands clinging tenaciously to her scalp. "I'd hoped getting her out and around others might give her enough change of scenery to perhaps jar her memory, but she's still trapped in the past." The woman smiled. "Oh, listen to me, not even introducing myself. I'm Valeria Clements, and this is my mother, Gertie."

Isabel frowned. "Clements. That name is familiar... Any relationship to Todd Clements?"

Valeria blinked and slowly nodded. "He was my older brother."

She grinned. "I'll be damn...darned. I dated Todd for a short time my junior year of high school."

The other woman seemed to be shocked, and she stared at Isabel. Suddenly, she smiled. "Isabel Campbell, right?"

Isabel nodded. "I'm afraid I don't remember you, but I guess you know me?"

"I was a freshman when you were a senior. I would have been in eighth grade when you dated Toddy." She frowned. "He died four years ago."

"Skydiving?" asked Isabel, resisting the urge to chuckle at how solemnly Valeria had broken news of his death, as though she'd spent the last sixty-plus years pining for her old boyfriend.

Valeria blinked. "Goodness, no. Wherever did you hear that? Toddy hated flying or heights. He never would have—"

Isabel hastily put up a hand. "My mistake. I must have been thinking of someone else." Valeria seemed to be lacking a sense of humor, but she was still better to talk to than the Senior Center Sally Minions.

"Oh, okay. Poor Toddy had a stroke. I guess it wasn't unexpected, but he'd been caring for Mother, and then Will took a turn, but he died a few months ago. It's just me and Mother now, all alone in that big house..." Valeria frowned. "It's quite taxing sometimes."

Isabel nodded, but her thoughts were on the big house. She scrunched her eyes and could vaguely recall the sprawling pale-yellow Victorian Todd had lived in. She'd visited once, and that had been it. Her eyes narrowed as they returned to Gertie. She remembered her now. Gertie had declared Isabel too wild and unladylike to be her son's friend, and that had pretty much been the end of the relationship.

Isabel hadn't been too heartbroken though. Todd had been milquetoast and a mama's boy. Unfortunately, she'd gotten with Andy a few weeks later, and other than having Willa, that had been the biggest mistake of her life.

"I always admired your spunk, Isabel. My mother said you didn't behave properly, but I liked that about you." Valeria blushed and laughed, as though admitting something embarrassing. "I wished back then I could be more like you."

"Er, thanks." How else to respond? It was awkward being praised just for being herself.

"This place is so dull." Valeria shook her head. "There just aren't many activities for someone like Mother."

"Or women our age who don't like scrapbooking or quilting."

Valeria smiled. "I enjoy scrapbooking, but my hands forced me to give it up. I can't hold scissors or a pen long enough these days." She lifted her hands as though to offer proof of the arthritis residing in her gnarled fingers.

"Right." Isabel shifted slightly. Valeria didn't seem like the most exciting company. "It's just you and Gertie now?"

Valeria nodded. "Yes. I never married, but Mother preferred to live with Toddy. He was her favorite." She sounded relieved, not bitter. "Then Will and his wife decided to move in to take care of her after Toddy's passing, but after Will's death, Marie went to live with her sister in Nebraska. At that point, there really was no choice except to move in with her."

"You could have put her in a home, or that retirement village."

Valeria blinked. "I couldn't do that. Mother would hate it, and it's in her will that all her money goes to charities if any of us abandon her in a home or force her to leave the Yellow Bliss."

Isabel blinked, trying to decide how to react to the information Valeria seemed to have unwittingly shared. Namely, she didn't want to take care of her mother, but financial concerns motivated her. She couldn't fault Valeria for being practical. Social security hardly went far these days, and if the other woman didn't have some independent investments, she probably needed the family money. Still, what a thing to admit to a virtual stranger.

She cleared her throat. "Yellow Bliss?"

Valeria sipped her coffee. "That's the name of the ancestral pile."

In Isabel's mind, the old Victorian hardly met the qualifications to be called something so grand, but she didn't argue. "I guess your mother must love it."

"Definitely, and it helps her maintain connections to her memories and the past." Valeria heaved a sigh. "It would be nice if she lived more in the present, but the doctor tells me that can't happen anymore. Still, I maintain hope…" She trailed off.

"I'm sorry for your difficulty."

Valeria smiled. "You're just as sweet as I always knew you'd be. Why don't you come over for tea in a couple of days, and I'll show you the Yellow Bliss?"

Isabel thought about refusing. She couldn't imagine Valeria was going to be that exciting of a companion. On the other hand, pickings were slim in Harrow Bay, and she was more colorful than the sheep at the Senior Center. "Why not?" Tea wasn't her thing, and she'd much prefer a stiff drink, but she could sit through a cup. Besides, she'd like to refresh her memory of the house. She didn't recall it having the name before, but it could be she and Todd just hadn't dated long enough for her to hear about the family.

Part of Isabel couldn't deny a surge of satisfaction at sitting in Gertie's parlor and drinking tea after the other woman had declared her not ladylike enough for Todd. It was a touch petty, and she doubted Gertie had any idea who she was, but Isabel liked the idea of returning in triumph to sit for tea and no longer be judged and found wanting. Gertie didn't seem capable of judging much of anything these days, but that was beside the point.

Chapter Three

Willa

"Do you want everything exactly where it was before?" asked Willa.

Patty paused in the middle of placing a box on the shelf in the back room. "What do you mean?"

"It's just, your organizing system from before was a little bit...creative."

Patty frowned as she came closer. "What are you trying to say, Willa?" The glint of teasing in her eyes was a marked contrast to the fake huff in her tone.

"I'm saying when it comes to running a craft store, you have your strengths, like knowing all the crafts. Perhaps I can help you back here."

Patty still looked vaguely offended, but mostly she appeared intrigued. "What do you have in mind?"

Willa shrugged. "I thought we might try alphabetical."

Patty frowned. "I'm not sure that makes any sense. Why wouldn't you keep the beads with the beads, or the yarn with the yarn, for example?"

Willa quickly put up a hand. She certainly didn't want to start a tiff with Patty when things were going so well. "I didn't mean separating them. I meant perhaps just organizing them alphabetically by type, so you could have your beads in alpha or alphanumeric order. I think it could make inventory and restocking a lot faster."

Patty blinked for a minute, and it was obvious that had never occurred to her. "I always just did them by color." She shrugged. "I guess we can give your way a try." She came closer, putting an arm around Willa's lower back. "You're not just a pretty face." She pressed a kiss to her cheek.

Willa blushed and giggled, feeling preposterous to hear the sound escape her at her age. She sounded ridiculously young and carefree, which was how Patty left her feeling most of the time. She certainly couldn't begrudge a girlish giggle now and then if it was a sign of how happy she was.

"This place is really starting to come back together." Patty took a step back and looked around, sighing with apparent satisfaction. "Frank always did his damnedest to ruin everything for me, and I guess that didn't end when he shuffled off his mortal coil."

Willa patted her girlfriend on the arm. "He definitely didn't get the best of you."

"Not that I'm happy with all the extra work he created, but at least the insurance company paid out quickly for the items that were destroyed. I still can't believe they bought that there was an earthquake localized under my store."

Willa shrugged. "It made as much sense as anything."

"I certainly couldn't tell them the ghost of my dead husband was harassing me by destroying my store, could I?"

Willa shifted, feeling uncomfortable with the topic. She'd been there and witnessed the whole thing, so it certainly wasn't a surprise to her, but that didn't mean she liked to talk about it or acknowledge certain truths about Harrow Bay. Sometimes, she wondered if she would still feel this way after she'd lived here for another twenty years.

Where her mother and daughter had adapted so easily, or seemingly had anyway, Willa still struggled to accept the supernatural was all around them, and she much preferred to live in denial. She was happy when most people indulged her most of the time. Patty didn't seem predisposed to do that though, and she was likely to talk openly about such things. Willa supposed she might stop if she asked her to, but she wasn't inclined to stifle Patty's communication either. They were building a relationship a day at a time, and that meant adapting to each other's quirks as well as finding all the pleasant things they had in common.

"Liesel is heading out of town," said Patty.

Willa looked up from opening a box of tiny pearl beads, currently confined to a clear acrylic case. "Oh? What's she doing?"

"She's going to meet up with some friends for a long weekend in Napa."

"That sounds fancy."

"It's an excuse to get drunk and have fun. We can do that right here in Harrow Bay." Patty winked.

Willa giggled again, wincing at how much she sounded like a teenager. "Yes, I suppose we can."

"I thought you might want to come over? She leaves Wednesday night. I'll make us some dinner."

Willa nodded, not quite paying attention. "That sounds fine."

"I thought I could make some oysters and lobster or something."

Willa looked up when she realized Patty was moving closer. "That sounds lovely. I'm sure you can get some fresh seafood at *Skip's*." It was a small seafood store right on the pier that served Harrow Bay, and the seafood was caught by local fishermen.

"No doubt." Patty heaved a soft sigh. "We could maybe have dessert?"

Willa nodded. "I'll never say no to chocolate cake."

"And then I thought maybe you could stay the night?"

Willa froze, looking at Patty in confusion for a moment before she realized exactly what Patty intended. She obviously wanted to take advantage of having an empty house, though Liesel lived in the apartment above the garage, and Willa wasn't certain how she felt about that. Her mouth went dry with nervousness, though there was definitely an air of anticipation hovering around the room, exuded by both of them. "You mean... Sleep over?"

"Yes, but I don't mean bring your own sleeping bag and spread it out on the floor." Patty bit her lip. "Is that too fast for you, Willa?"

Willa waved a hand. "Of course not. I'm totally fine with that." Did she sound as unbelievable to Patty as she did to herself?

Patty sent her a considering look, and she frowned slightly. "I mean, there's no pressure. Whatever happens happens, but Liesel won't be there, so if something happens, at least we know we have private time for it to happen."

A nervous titter escaped Willa, and she sought solace in humor. "We've established that something might happen then."

Patty grinned. "Yes, and that can be as vague or all-encompassing as necessary."

Willa smiled at her, but the smile gradually faded away as Patty turned from the back room to enter the main part of the shop when the bell on the door rang to indicate there was a visitor. She lingered for a moment longer, her fingers going through the motions of putting beads on the shelves, but her brain was otherwise engaged.

She wasn't certain why she was so blindsided by Patty's suggestion that they might try intimacy. They'd been together for weeks, and they'd been friends before that. In some ways, it felt like dizzying speed, but in others, she was impatient to pass the first real hurdle in the relationship—aside from their breakup prompted by Willa's inability to accept her feelings for the other woman.

Now that they were past that, intimacy seemed like the next big hurdle to face, and Willa was embarrassed that she didn't really have a clue how to proceed. She could leave a certain amount of imagination, and she imagined pretty well, especially when she thought about Patty at night, but it wasn't the same as doing. Elton had been her only lover, and there'd been a couple of boyfriends before him, but she had never so much as dipped a pinky in the other side of the pool until Patty. Now she was contemplating jumping into the deep end in her birthday suit.

Realizing she was hiding in the back room, she put aside the box she'd been working on and went into the main part of the store. Patty was checking out a handsome man in his fifties, and he had several packages of embroidery floss in front of him. She approached, and he smiled at her. She shivered slightly, uncertain why a chill went through her. Willa's professional smile she had in place wilted slightly, but she managed to say, "Hello," in a semi-normal sounding tone.

He nodded his head at her. "You're Sheriff Shaw's mother, aren't you?"

She nodded. "I'm afraid I don't know who you are though, sir."

"I'm Ryland Santiri. I own the Italian restaurant in town." When he smiled again, she realized his canines were just a bit longer than typical, and they seemed to have a slightly sharper edge.

She glanced at them for a moment before prying away her gaze and taking the hand he extended. "It's lovely to meet you. You have excellent eggplant parmigiana."

He gave her a cryptic smile. "It's an old family recipe. Old country, you could say."

She nodded. "I guess it's been handed down for generations?"

Ryland stared at her for a moment and then laughed. "Yes, I guess you could say that." He paid for his purchases and wished them a good day before exiting the store.

"Was he buying that for his wife or girlfriend?"

Patty giggled, now the one sounding like a teenager, and nudged her lightly with her hip. "Why? Are you interested in him?"

Willa flushed and started fluttering her hand in front of her face. "Of course not. He's young enough to be my..." She trailed off with a frown. "Well, he's certainly several years younger than me anyway."

Patty laughed then, a virtual guffaw that had her leaning against the counter for support. Willa put her hands on her hips and stared at her girlfriend. "What's so funny?"

"Uh, just that he's about five hundred years older than you, Willa."

Willa frowned. "You mean metaphorically?"

"I mean literally." Patty practically howled with laughter for a moment, necessitating the need to wipe her eyes before she could continue. "He's a vampire, hon. When he mentioned the old country and family recipe, he likely got it himself from his oldest ancestors and brought it with him."

Willa gasped, putting a hand to her mouth. "But I've eaten at their restaurant."

Patty frowned. "So? It's not like you can become a vampire by eating food they prepare. Don't be a bigot, love."

Willa glared at her. "I hardly think it's a bigot to be concerned about eating at vampiric establishments." She closed her eyes for a moment, taking a deep breath. How strange her life had become since coming to Harrow Bay. She frowned. "I don't understand. Italian food is full of garlic."

Patty started howling with laughter again before finally settling down and taking a deep breath to answer. "I love that that's your takeaway. It's just one of the things I adore about you, Willa." She leaned forward and pressed a kiss to her cheek.

Willa was still a little irritated, feeling like she was the subject of mockery, but she could see there was no vicious intent behind it. Patty was truly amused, and Willa decided not to be offended. "I'm sorry, but that's the way my mind works. How can they serve good, authentic Italian food and be vampires?"

"I don't understand all the rules myself, but I think if they are vulnerable to garlic, it's only if it enters the bloodstream. It's an anticoagulant... Or is it a coagulant?" She shrugged. "Either way, it changes the chemistry of their blood or something. I'm sure they have their human employees prep the garlic and taste anything with it in the dish. You've had the food, so you know it's authentic."

Willa nodded. "Elton and I did take a trip to Italy when Jody and Ronnie were little." She blinked, pushing back the memories of that special time. "So, who was the thread for?"

Patty closed the register, which had still been open due to her laughing fit. She took a moment to blow her nose, and then she said, "They were for Ryland, of course. He tells me he finds embroidery very soothing, and it reminds him of the days when he used to watch his mother and sister work on the tapestries."

Willa blinked. "So, he's a five-hundred-year-old vampire who cooks authentic Italian food and dabbles in embroidery?" She shook her head. "Things certainly are different here."

"They are, but that's one of the amazing things about Harrow Bay." Patty leaned closer. "It's not my favorite part though."

Willa looked at her. "What is?"

"You are." Patty leaned forward and brushed her lips against hers. "I'm looking forward to Wednesday night, regardless of whatever happens or doesn't happen, okay? I don't want you to spend all week stressing about it."

Willa tensed slightly, but she frowned. "I won't. I'm not concerned at all."

Patty gave her a look full of disbelief, but her tone was gentle when she said, "Of course you aren't." With a sigh, she pulled back. "I guess we should finish organizing the back room."

"I guess so. We don't have anything else to do."

Patty seemed on the verge of suggesting something, but the bell rang again, heralding the arrival of new customers, and it was the beginning of an onslaught of women and men who'd been denied their crafts during the two weeks Patty had needed to restore order to her store and reopen.

Willa was relieved to have something to focus on, because each time she thought about the approaching night with Patty, nerves clenched her stomach into a tight ball, and she had the urge to throw up. It wasn't that Patty made her nauseated. She was just nervous. There was clearly a fine line between love and nausea.

Chapter Four

Jody

A couple of mornings later, Jody entered the kitchen to the welcome smell of coffee and the sight of Daphne sitting at the table with Gram. She went to the coffeepot and poured herself a cup before coming to sit with them. "I'm surprised to see you up so early." She addressed that to Daphne.

Her friend shrugged. "I had a little trouble sleeping."

"Nightmares?" asked Jody.

"Snoring." Daphne grinned at her. "You still have that habit."

Jody sniffed. "You have yet to prove that assertion."

"I'll have to remember to record it sometime." Daphne stirred cream into her coffee.

Jody took the container of cream as soon as Daphne was finished and added a generous dose to her coffee. "I'm sorry I've been neglecting you the last couple of days." Surprisingly, Harrow Bay had been full of frenetic activity the past two days. They were all small cases, but it kept her hopping, especially since Bob Smith, the replacement deputy who was supposed to fill in for Michael during his vacation, had been delayed in his arrival.

Things seemed to finally be settling down again, so she said, "Barring any unexpected craziness popping up, I should be home at the usual time tonight. Would you like to go out for dinner?"

Daphne stirred her coffee before licking the spoon and setting it aside. "I'd love to, but I've already made plans."

Jody frowned. "I didn't know you knew anyone else here."

"You know me. I can make friends wherever I go." Daphne waved her hand in a blithe fashion. "It comes easily to me."

Jody nodded, recalling how Daphne had marched up to her on their first day of kindergarten and told her they were going to do jump rope together. Jody had been somewhat shy at the time, so she'd gone along with Daphne's plan, and they'd been inseparable ever since. Even when truly separated by long distances, they maintained their friendship in one form or another.

"Tomorrow though?" asked Daphne.

Jody nodded. "Yeah, that sounds like a plan." She had to bite down the urge to question Daphne about her date. At least, she assumed it was a date. It could just be someone Daphne had connected with and whom she shared a common interest. Her best friend truly had no difficulty making new friends, but Jody suspected if that had been the case, Daphne would have invited her along.

It sounded like an actual date, so she was a little nervous on her friend's behalf. With Harrow Bay, and assuming the date came from the limited dating pool around there, Daphne could be getting far more than she expected.

She resisted the urge to warn her, because that would lead to an uncomfortable conversation, and she wasn't certain Daphne would believe her anyway. It all sounded quite fantastical, so she could hardly blame her friend for questioning her sanity if she had to tell her about Harrow Bay. For now, it seemed prudent to hang back and just watch the situation, to ensure Daphne didn't end up with someone dangerous.

After a quick breakfast, Jody headed to the office. After the last two days that were full of adrenaline, it was nice to settle back into a quieter routine. She was heading to her office, planning to work on spell memorization and practice some of the spells when she ran into Beez. He had one of Dora's donuts in his talons, and he looked like he was deeply focused on something as he rushed past her.

"'Morning, Jody," he called as he walked past.

"Good morning, Beez. What're you up to so early?"

"Microfiche."

Jody frowned. "You're still working on that project?" She'd kind of suggested it out of a desire to needle him, but he seemed to be sticking with it. "You don't actually have to do that to stay here." Guilt forced her conscience to admit the truth, though she hated to since he was being useful and industrious.

He shrugged a shoulder. "I don't really mind. It's kind of interesting seeing all the history of the town. I mean, I was here for a lot of it, but it's only been the last sixty years or so that I've lived at the Sheriff's Station and had more of a conduit to what's going on. Before that, a lot of the town goings-on were shielded from me, since I was living in the old Methodist church's basement."

Jody frowned. "Wait a minute. The church let you live in their basement before you lived in the Sheriff's Station?"

He nodded. "At least until a storm came and damaged the building so much that it had to be torn down."

Jody shook her head in wonder. "How in the world did you talk them into letting you do that? You're sort of in the competing business, aren't you?"

He sniffed at her. "I'm not in any business except my own business, Jody. You should know that about me by now." His eyes gleamed with avarice.

She nodded in a placating fashion, though she sometimes thought part of Beez's self-centered attitude was mainly for show. "Seriously, how did you persuade the minister to let you stay?"

"Ministers," said Beez. "I lived there for a few hundred years off and on. I just explained to them we had a common enemy."

Her brow crept toward her hairline. "Are you talking about Luc?"

He nodded.

Jody frowned. "I didn't realize you considered Luc an enemy. I just thought you made him angry."

"With him, that's sometimes all it takes to become his enemy forever. I have no love for him anyway, so we struck a deal, and the church let me stay in exchange for protecting it."

Jody frowned. "Is your magic up to that task?"

He didn't really answer. The shuffling of his feet was the answer required, allowing her to infer that he'd implied greater capabilities than he actually had, and the Methodists had gone for it. She was still frankly shocked they'd agreed to the arrangement, but it was in the past, so she couldn't find the ministers to question why they had believed Beez, even if she cared enough to do so. Which she most definitely didn't. "Well, I'll leave you to the microfiche then, and I have some spells to memorize and practice."

"I'd think you'd be done with all that by now, Jody."

Jody shrugged. "I want to make sure I've mastered everything. Some of the spells are quite difficult to memorize, and the slightest missed inflection can cause everything to go wrong."

Beez nodded his agreement, but he didn't speak again. Instead, he crammed the other half of the donut in his mouth, lifted his hand in a wave of parting, and disappeared into the back room. If he could be believed, he was going to the microfiche machine to convert the old articles into digital files. She had no reason to doubt him, other than he was a demon. She didn't think he was necessarily always rigid about telling the truth, but she doubted he was fibbing to her about working on the microfiche either. He had no reason to.

The day remained as uneventful as it had started out, and as the end of her shift approached, Jody's cell phone rang. A glance at the caller ID revealed it was Gram, so she hit the speakerphone. "What is it, Gram?"

"Willa called to say she's working late. I guess they're having some trouble restoring all the items to the shelves, and she wants to put in some kind a new inventory system that Patty seems to be struggling with."

"I'm surprised Patty is letting her experiment with her store."

Isabel chuckled. "She probably realizes Willa's good at all those tedious details. She's always been a detail-oriented person."

"True, unless they are uncomfortable details she doesn't want to confront." Jody laughed softly. "What do you want to do about dinner then?"

"That's why I'm calling. I placed an order with *Santiri's*, so I thought you could pick it up on your way home?"

Jody grimaced and hesitated. As much as she hated to admit it, she disliked going into the vampires' restaurant. Being around them at all made her uneasy, but she straightened her shoulders and decided she was being ridiculous. "I hope you ordered me eggplant parmigiana."

"Of course, I did. What else would you get at an Italian restaurant?" Isabel sounded like she was smacking her lips together. "I also got a side of spicy clam sauce."

Jody groaned. "I guess we'd better open the windows and break out the gas masks."

"When it comes to being a comedian, you're a pretty good sheriff." Isabel cackled. "So, you'll pick up the food?"

"Sure. It sounds as good as anything, and I don't have to cook it."

After hanging up with Gram, she locked the book in her desk and decided it was close enough to the end of her shift to leave. She was only shaving off five minutes, and she left the station a few minutes later.

It didn't take long to reach *Santiri's*, and she pulled into the parking lot. It was already starting to get busy, though it was just a little past five, but that happened in a small town where dining options were limited.

She climbed out of the vehicle, used the fob to lock it, and entered the restaurant all in under a minute. Even with the slight line waiting to be seated, it didn't take long for the hostess to acknowledge her. "A table for one?"

"No. I'm here to pick up a carryout order for Isabel Campbell."

The hostess looked down for a moment and then nodded. "Give me just a second to grab that."

Jody nodded and moved over to the wall, reaching into her purse to remove her credit card. As she glanced up through the ornate carvings etched in the wood panels, she got a glimpse of a familiar face sitting in the restaurant. With a frown, she moved from the front, ignoring the glares of a couple of people waiting to be seated, and walked into the dining room. She stood near the table where Daphne sat with a menu open in front of her. "You're having dinner here?"

Daphne stiffened, but then she looked up and smiled. "Hey, I didn't know you were going to be here."

"Gram wanted Italian, and she ordered spicy clam sauce."

Daphne wrinkled her nose. "Oh, great."

"We'll open the windows. It'll be fine." Jody thought about sitting down, but she didn't want to intrude. It was odd to feel that way with her friend, but it was clear Daphne was waiting for someone. "Is your date running late?"

"Not really. He has to work in between. I'm more like his guest than his date." Daphne looked uncertain for a moment. "I guess you could join me if you want?"

It was obvious she would be a fifth wheel if she did, so Jody shook her head. "Who is this mystery man though?"

Before Daphne could answer, Ryland appeared then, placing a lobster tail surrounded by fennel and other ingredients Jody didn't have a chance to identify in front of Daphne with a flourish. "For your starter, Daph," he said with a grin. Then he looked up, caught sight of Jody, and looked a little uncomfortable. "Hello, Sheriff Shaw. Are you joining Daphne this evening?"

For a second, she was tempted to do so, just to protect her friend. Ultimately, she knew she couldn't though. How could she explain feeling the need to protect Daphne from Ryland without telling her exactly what he was? The confusion in the situation made her head start to pound, and she rubbed at her eyelids before shaking her head. "No. I was just here to pick up a take-out and saw Daphne seated here."

"There's plenty if you want to join her." Ryland sounded gracious, but she couldn't help feeling like he really wanted her to leave. Was that because he wanted Daphne to himself, or did he have more nefarious purposes in mind? She hated to be suspicious, but it was sort of her job, and he was a vampire.

"Nah, she has to get home to her gram."

Daphne had spoken firmly, and Jody nodded. "I really do." Feeling a little awkward, she shifted in her Rockports and said, "I hope you both have a good time tonight. Make sure you keep her safe, Ryland." It was meant to be a lighthearted parting, but it came out with an underlying note of seriousness that caused the vampire's unpigmented eyes to widen, and he cleared his throat.

"Of course. I'll make sure she gets home safely."

Jody couldn't mother-hen all night, so she nodded and parted from them, claimed the bag from the hostess, who was waiting impatiently, and passed over her card all within the space of a few minutes. Even as she walked out of the restaurant, she was concerned that Daphne was having dinner with Ryland, at least amid his normal duties. She tried not to worry, but it was difficult to know her friend was socializing with a creature who could drain her blood and leave her dry—or even worse, convert her.

She knew she had to trust Daphne's judgment, which was normally pretty sound. She was only nervous because Daphne didn't know the whole picture, and Jody wasn't certain how to explain it to her without revealing the truth of Harrow Bay.

Instead, she did her best to dismiss her concerns, reminding herself Daphne was a grown woman who'd managed to take care of herself this long, and Ryland seemed reasonably honorable, especially for a vampire. It was a situation that warranted monitoring, but there was nothing she could do now anyway.

When she arrived home, she was surprised to find Drake sitting in the living room with Gram. "I didn't know you'd be here. I'm sorry, but I didn't grab you any food."

Isabel cackled. "Yes, you did. He's been here for a while, waiting for you. I called in an order for him too."

"Eggplant parmigiana?" asked Jody as she took the bag into the kitchen, and they followed.

"He's a philistine. He wanted some squid dish." Gram clicked her tongue. "Still, I can't argue with the boy. He is half-demon."

Jody laughed at how carelessly her grandmother referenced that. It was a subject Willa had been careful to avoid. When Drake had shown up for Halloween in his demon form, her mother had missed it since she'd been out, and though Jody hadn't made any attempt to hide Drake's nature, admittedly, she hadn't blurted it out to her mother either.

Gram was a different story though. She had taken it all in stride, not changing how she treated Drake and showing no visible fear of him, to Jody's relief. She knew he could be big and intimidating, and he was a fierce bounty hunter for Hell, but there was nothing fearful about him to her, so she was glad Gram didn't fear him either.

Soon enough, they had dinner distributed and tucked in. The eggplant parmigiana was as good as any she'd ever had, and Jody realized she'd have to go to *Santiri's* more often if she wanted the dish. Heavens knew she couldn't reproduce it well enough on her own. Besides, it wouldn't hurt to keep a closer eye on the vampires, especially if Daphne was associating with one while she was in town. "Do you know Ryland very well?" She looked at Drake as she asked.

He shrugged. "He's a vampire, and he cooks really well."

Jody looked down at her meal. "He probably didn't cook this himself, but it is his recipe?" That part was issued as a question, since she couldn't imagine it would be anyone else's.

Drake shrugged. "Whoever came up with it, I'm glad they did." He seemed to be enjoying his squid cooked in some kind of spicy tomato base and plopped on top of pappardelle pasta.

"He's never caused much trouble around here then?"

Drake shrugged again. "Not as far as I know. There are a few ferals here and there..."

Jody nodded, shuddering as she recalled her first interaction with the vampires, when Val had gone feral and destroyed the UPS driver before Ryland had put him down. It had been a barbaric way to proceed, but seeing the creature in its pathetic state, and realizing how dangerous he was like that, she hadn't had a better idea, so she'd agreed to allow the vampires to handle their ferals. To her knowledge, there hadn't been more incidents since then, and she hoped it stayed like that for the rest of her career as sheriff of Harrow Bay.

"Why do you ask? Has he caught your eye?" Drake appeared to be trying to tease her, but there was definitely a note of jealousy in his tone.

She reached over and squeezed his hand. "Vampires aren't my type. I prefer demons."

He rolled his eyes, but he looked unaccountably pleased with her answer, and she had to bite back a grin at his reaction. "I was just wondering about him. Daphne's having dinner with him."

Gram frowned. "With a bloodsucker?"

"That's sort of an offensive term," said Drake in a conversational style. "They get a little testy about that, especially since the vampires in Harrow Bay only drink animal blood."

"They're still bloodsuckers." Isabel shrugged. "What's the point in mincing words?"

"Civility?" suggested Jody. "They probably don't like to be reminded of their circumstances."

Isabel snorted. "Who does? It's not like I enjoy mine. My only social outlet appears to be a bunch of old people, and tomorrow, I'm going for tea." She snorted as she shook her head. "Me, going for tea? It's absolutely preposterous, don't you think?"

"I don't know. Are you going to get a fancy hat and wear white gloves?" Jody grinned as her grandmother stuck out her tongue. "I'll admit afternoon tea is more Mom's thing than yours, but you should give it a fair chance. You might enjoy it."

"It's overly fussy for me, but at least Valeria seems a nice enough woman. She's burdened with her mother, who seems nuttier than a fruitcake."

Jody winced. "Your sensitivity is as overwhelming as ever, Gram."

Isabel didn't let the admonishment bother her. She just shrugged again. "It's the truth. The woman was staring at the wall and talking to herself. When I get old, if I'm like that..." She trailed off with a shake of her head.

Jody resisted the urge to point out that many people would consider Isabel old already at seventy-nine, because she understood her grandmother didn't feel that. Despite her physical age, Isabel had a youthful spirit, and she couldn't imagine that would change even as her grandmother got older.

Besides, she'd like to think the old lady had at least another twenty or thirty years hanging about, so she had plenty of time to get older, though Jody hoped many of the more common perils of aging skipped over her grandmother. As it was, Isabel had a hard enough time dealing with bad eyesight, arthritic knees, and high blood pressure. She frowned. "Gram, where are your glasses?"

Isabel muttered something, but she reached into her pocket and put them on. "Happy now, dear?" Her biting tone revealed she wasn't.

"You know the optometrist said you have to wear them all the time to get benefit from them."

"I am, I am. I just forgot to put them on when I washed my face before dinner."

Jody gave her a suspicious look, but there was no way to disprove the claim, so she simply nodded.

After dinner, they retired to the living room, and Isabel apparently decided to be tactful. She gave an exaggerated yawn. "I think I'll have an early night. You two have fun." There was a suggestive gleam in her eyes, and she winked as she got to her feet.

Jody resisted the urge to blush at her grandmother's not-so-subtle proposal that they engage in indecent activities. She had no objection to doing that, but she wasn't about to confirm it for her grandmother. Not that Gram was likely genuinely interested in what she planned to do with Drake. Even the few times he'd slept over when they were under the effects of the love spell, Gram hadn't blinked an eye to learn he'd stayed overnight, but she hadn't requested details either.

After Isabel had left, Jody curled up on the couch and laid her head on Drake's arm. "Do you want to watch TV or something?"

"Sure, but nothing too taxing on my brain. It's been a long day, and I still have a trip to make tonight."

She frowned. "Tonight? Where?"

"It's an establishment you wouldn't know. It's mostly frequented by demons, and it's a hundred miles from here. I'll have to ride straight through once I leave here."

Jody shifted slightly so she can look up at him, making no attempt to mask her concern. "It's a long drive at night on your motorcycle. Do you want me to take you in the SUV?"

He shook his head. "You have to work early tomorrow, and it's pretty routine. I go to the place probably a few times a year looking for information. I'm hoping Honsiu decided to take up residence around there, or at least he's visited, so I can get a lock on his location."

"You sound weary."

"More like wary, though I am tired. Honsiu is nothing to mess around with. He's not like a typical demon possession, and he wasn't a human that was twisted into a demon through punishment. He was born a demon, or created, I guess you could say. Luc went through a dabbling phase when he was first ejected from Heaven, deciding he wanted to be the new god of his domain. He created a plethora of demons, at least until he got tired of playing the creator. Honsiu was one of the first, and he's also one of the worst."

Seeing Drake's visible unease contributed to her own, and Jody snuggled closer as she put an arm over his stomach. "Are you sure you don't need some help?"

"I'll call you if I need you, but this really isn't your problem, Jody."

She frowned. "It is if he comes to Harrow Bay."

Drake nodded, clearly conceding the point. "It's pretty unlikely though. He crawled out of the Hell gate here, and I imagine Luc's magic affects him, but not to the same extent as the usual escapee. No doubt, he has a wider range of freedom and moved away from the area by now. I can't imagine him sticking around for long."

"What did he do?"

"In addition to the usual demon things, Luc particularly wants him back because he decided to leave Hell without permission. It's not like you can just come and go as you please, unless you have certain special dispensations."

"Like yours?" Jody patted his stomach lightly. It was more of a soothing gesture for herself than him, and she realized she was on edge.

He nodded. "I'm not actually a demon, per se. I have demon heritage, but I don't really fall under his purview as much, so I'm more resistant to his power. I follow his rules because I choose to, and because I'm sort of stuck between two worlds, and he offers me a better chance to use my unique skillset." He chuckled, and his eyes flashed red for a moment.

She smiled, trying to hide her nervousness. "Are you sure you don't need some backup though? What about another demon hunter?"

He shrugged. "That's always an option, but I hope I won't need it. I'm not sure Honsiu is even in my sector, but that's why I've been run ragged, making sure. So far, he's been quiet and off the radar. A quiet demon isn't necessarily behaving himself. You can't trust a demon or drop your guard with them."

"Except you." She snuggled closer.

"Except me," he agreed. "I'm different though. I'm only half-demon, and my soul isn't as dark and twisted. I'm a product of the circumstances of my birth, not something created by my own evil actions."

She laid her head firmly over his heart, listening to the steady thump of the beat beneath her ear. "I can't really picture you doing anything evil."

"Don't make me sound like a saint either. I am a demon, or at least half-demon." He sounded offended.

She shrugged. "Still, you're not the evil type."

He looked slightly disgruntled. "I can be completely evil."

Jody shook her head. "I don't believe it." She let out a startled gasp and then a giggle a moment later as he pinched her on the bottom and then started to tickle her. "Stop. Let go of me."

He continued to tickle mercilessly. "Am I evil?"

Jody shook her head, battling to get out words through her laughter. "Not even close."

He increased the speed of his tickling and started branching outward from her sides to tickle her back and her stomach as well. "How about now?"

"Maybe a little evil." It was difficult to get out any of the words through her laughter. As he continued to tickle her, her sides started to ache from laughing and from his tickling, and she struggled to squirm away. "Okay, I concede you're evil."

"It's about time you realize the full breadth and awesomeness of my powers." He stopped tickling her and pulled her onto his lap completely, holding her in his arms.

She leaned against him, nuzzling his throat and gently nibbling on the skin there. "You're so evil." She said it in a condescending fashion, deliberately over-exaggerating her tone.

"Damned right I am," he said with a satisfied chuckle as he smacked her on the butt again, but his hands were gentle as they curved to her body, holding her against him.

Jody closed her eyes, enjoying the moment and not ruining it by continuing to tease him about his lack of evil aptitude. She supposed he could be quite fierce, and she'd seen him in battle a few times, but she couldn't help thinking her lover lacked that completely ruthless edge that must be inherent to most demons. At least when it came to her, and the people of the town, he was anything but ruthless. He was practically a kitten, though she wasn't dumb enough to tell him that, since she didn't want to endure another onslaught of tickling.

Chapter Five

Jody

Drake was still there when Daphne returned from her date, looking radiant. Jody had seen that often enough to know it'd been a good evening, but that didn't mean it would lead to anything more serious. She smiled and scooted over closer to Drake when Daphne dropped onto the cushion beside her. "How was your date with Ryland?"

Daphne sighed as she leaned back, kicking up her feet on the ottoman. "Marvelous. He's so gentlemanly, and there's such an old-world charm about him. He's practically medieval."

"Or perhaps at least Renaissance," said Jody, tongue-in-cheek.

If Daphne thought her tone was odd, she showed no indication. "You could be right." She seemed thoughtful. "He's into so many things, you know?"

Jody shook her head. "I really don't. I don't know Ryland well at all."

Daphne shrugged. "He cooks, he paints, and he even embroiders."

"It takes a secure man to tell you that on the first date," said Drake, looking like he might laugh.

Daphne glared at him. "I think it's marvelous that he's so talented. He has those amazing long fingers. Just thinking about them..." She trailed off with a clear shiver of delight.

The idea put Jody's teeth on edge, because she could all too clearly picture them forming sharp talons as the feral vampire had displayed. The idea of Ryland's fingers moving over anything in passion, but especially a warm and vibrant human like her best friend, was unsettling.

"The best part is, he doesn't seem to have any ex-wives or children hiding about."

Jody laughed. "Who are you kidding? You're still in your stepkids' lives."

Daphne shrugged again. "I am, and they're all wonderful young adults, but they aren't my kids. That's the difference, as I'm sure you understand. They can come to me if they need something, but they aren't reliant on me to keep them alive. You know me. I can't even keep a goldfish living."

"Children are considerably more complex," said Drake. "I think they tend to give you cues when they're hungry and need attention."

Daphne waved a slender wrist. "Yes, I suppose, but I was never terribly interested in picking up on their cues. Neither was Jody."

Jody nodded. "Do you remember that one weekend we babysat for your neighbor?"

After a moment, Daphne looked horrified. "The ones with the triplets of terror?"

Jody nodded, able to laugh about it now, but it had been a traumatic experience at the time.

Drake frowned. "What did I miss?"

"Just evil incarnate, compacted into three little terrors. It was the first and last time either one of us ever tried to babysit." Daphne leaned forward, taking Jody's last half-glass of wine and draining it in one gulp. "Put me off having children for life."

Jody looked at Drake, who was unexpectedly serious. "Is that what you have no children too, Jody?"

She shook her head and laughed. "Not at all. I mean, those kids were pretty much the poster children for why you would want to take birth control, but I'm sure not every kid is like that."

"People do tend to like their own better."

"Or their stepkids, at least in moderation." Daphne smiled as she said that.

"So, what made you not want to have children?"

Jody frowned at the unexpected gravity underlying Drake's tone.

Daphne apparently thought the question was for her. "I don't know. I guess the situations were just never right enough to feel like I wanted to bring a baby into them. Or I married a man who already had a kid or two, and he wasn't looking to add to the family. I'm terribly vain, and I like having a nice figure. I didn't really want to go through childbirth, and I'm a dreadful baby about pain."

"That she is."

Drake looked at her. "What about you, Jody?" He was obviously struggling to sound casual.

She hesitated for a moment and lifted a shoulder in a shrug. "There isn't one single, defining reason why I don't want kids, Drake. I guess like Daphne, partly the situation never worked out where I felt like it was a good time to have them, but I've never really felt a strong maternal drive either. I've been pretty focused on my career, and having a child would just distract me from that. I'm probably way too old now anyway, and that ship has sailed."

"Sailed and exploded," said Daphne with a giggle. She sounded the slightest bit tipsy, indicating the last half of Jody's wine wasn't her first of the evening. Daphne looked at Drake then. "Do you want kids or something? You're getting a little old for that, aren't you?"

Drake frowned in irritation. "I'm about Jody's age."

"Yes, and you certainly seem to have aged well. So has Ryland."

Jody sighed at Daphne's obvious enchantment with the vampire. She still wasn't sure what she could do about it though.

Drake yawned and stretched. "It's getting late, and I know you have to work tomorrow. I have things to do as well."

She knew where he had to go, and she squeezed his hand. "Be careful while you're there and when you're out hunting, okay?"

The corners of his eyes crinkled when he smiled widely as he leaned over and pressed a kiss to her mouth. It was little more than a brush of his lips against hers, and he was likely inhibited by Daphne's presence. So was Jody, so she didn't object to the light kiss. Instead, she trailed behind him to the door, not at all surprised when he turned and pressed her against the wall, claiming a far more passionate kiss before pulling away. She put a hand on his cheek. "You will be careful, won't you? This Honsiu guy sounds pretty scary."

He rolled his massive shoulders. "I'm always careful, and I have more reasons than ever to make it back in one piece." He stroked her palm for a moment before letting go of her hand. "Good night, Jody."

"Good night, Drake." She watched him from the open door until he exited her house, walked down the stairs, and was soon seated on Evita. When the motorcycle roared to life, she closed the door and locked it. She waited until she heard him drive away before turning off the light and going back into the living room.

Daphne was snuggled up on the couch, her head on a throw pillow, and she'd claimed the throw from the back to drape over herself.

"Don't you want to come upstairs?"

Daphne waved a hand. "No, I'm fine here. Just too much work to walk all the way upstairs." She yawned.

Jody was alarmed at her sudden lack of energy, and she leaned down. Without explanation, she brushed back Daphne's hair, checking each side of her neck for fang marks.

Daphne's eyes opened, and the brown orbs stared up at her in confusion. "What in the world are you doing?"

Jody stumbled to a halt, searching for an explanation. "I was just making sure you're okay." Seeing Daphne still looking confused, she said, "I mean that you had enough air and everything." It sounded lame even to her own ears, but she wasn't certain how to explain her fear that Ryland had turned her friend into an after-dinner nosh.

Daphne shook her head. "Don't get weird on me, babe."

"I'm just worried about you. How much do you really know about this Ryland?"

Daphne frowned. "I know he's handsome, successful, and doesn't have the usual baggage. His past is practically squeaky clean compared to all the men I've been with before."

Jody couldn't help snorting. "Somehow, I doubt that." If anything, he was likely to have a far more extensive past than any man Daphne had been with before, simply because he was at least five hundred years old. One didn't live that long without accumulating an assortment of baggage.

Daphne's eyes opened wide, seeming more aware. "Seriously, do you have a problem with Ryland?"

Jody hesitated, wishing she could figure out how to verbalize her concerns without sounding like a madwoman. "I just don't know if you can trust him. When I first came to town, there was some trouble at his compound."

"What kind of trouble?"

"Murder," said Jody softly.

Daphne's eyes widened. "Are you telling me Ryland is a murderer?"

Reluctantly, Jody shook her head. "No, he wasn't the murderer. In fact, he was the one who handled the situation... I mean, he let us know about it and turned in his person." The whole explanation sounded halting, but Daphne didn't seem to notice.

"Then what's the problem? It's not like he murdered someone, and if he cooperated with your investigation, why are you suspicious of him?"

"It's not so much who he is as what he is."

Daphne gasped. "Are you expressing some sort of prejudice against him because he's Italian?"

Jody blinked. "Of course not. That's ridiculous."

"I would think so too, but it sure sounds it's what your problem is with him. Unless..." She trailed off with her gaze narrowed. "You didn't get serious about Drake when you first moved to town. Were you and Ryland involved first?"

Jody scowled. "Of course not."

Daphne was still staring at her, eyes narrowed in suspicion. "I'm not entirely sure I believe you. Maybe you wanted to start something with him, and he wasn't interested. I can see why that might bother you, even if you're with Drake now. If that's the case, you should just say so, and I'll back off."

Jody snorted. "You wouldn't back off even if that were the case—which it isn't."

Daphne rolled her eyes and turned over, her back facing Jody. "I'm going to get some sleep. If you want to talk about this in the morning, we can then, but I hope you'll be over your jealousy by then. I don't know why you'd care, since you have Drake, and he seems practically perfect for you. Bruised ego, maybe?"

Jody let out a cry of frustration, but she didn't pursue the topic. "Good night." She was a little stiff with the words, and Daphne was just as stiff when she reiterated them, but Jody turned and went upstairs before it could escalate to an argument, and she might say something she'd regret. She was no closer to making Daphne understand why she was concerned, and she still didn't know how to broach the topic with her friend, who was only passing through Harrow Bay. If she hadn't hooked up with Ryland, it would've been a much simpler visit all around.

***

Jody went down early the next morning, planning to be the first in the office as usual, aside from Beez. If she made it early enough, Ollie would still be there, which was hardly a bright point, but she could endure him for a little while. She stifled a yawn as she slipped past the couch and into the kitchen.

She hadn't slept well, and as she started to flip on the light, she let out a startled squeal as the one above the sink went on first. She put a hand on her chest, as though to hold in her thumping heart, and shot a reflexive look at the couch. She hadn't noticed when tiptoeing past in the dark that Daphne had abandoned it. It was her friend who had turned on the light, and Jody recognized the scent of coffee brewing as her senses returned to normal, getting over the fright of the unexpected encounter in the kitchen.

"There's coffee," said Daphne. Her tone was somewhat conciliatory.

Jody cleared her throat as she moved closer with a nod. "Yeah, I see that." She inhaled. "Oh, did you brew up some of your special stuff?"

"Straight from Brazil, when I was there for Carnival."

Jody poured a cup, and they moved to the table by unspoken agreement. There was no food, but Jody wasn't quite ready to eat. After her restless night, she was still feeling tense, and she was unhappy with the distance between them.

"I'm sorry," said Daphne.

Just a second after her, Jody said, "I'm sorry."

They looked at each other and shared an awkward laugh. "I guess I was overly sensitive. I really like Ryland, and you usually don't like the guys I'm with. Unfortunately, you're usually right about them too, and I really don't want you to be right about Ryland. He's such a sweet man, and I think he and I could have something special."

Jody nodded slowly. "It could be that you might be able to. I just want you to get to know him well before you rush into anything. I don't know much about him either, and I'm certainly not jealous of the bond you guys are developing or something. I'm just worried about you."

Daphne pulled a face. "With good reason. I certainly have a history of rushing into unsuitable relationships. It seems to be my special talent from time to time."

"Time after time is more like it," said Jody with a small grin over the rim of her coffee cup.

Daphne rolled her eyes, but she laughed. "I guess that's fair. I really do appreciate your concern, but I'm sure you know I'm a grown woman. I have a propensity to make mistakes, but Ryland feels different."

"I can't argue with that. I don't think he's like anyone you've ever dated before." She couldn't keep the hint of pensiveness from her tone.

Daphne seemed like she might argue for a moment, but then she shrugged. "No, I don't suppose he is. I'm looking forward to getting to know him better."

"In that case, I'll try to make an effort to get to know him better too. I just haven't had much opportunity since coming to Harrow Bay. Work keeps me busy." She glanced at the clock on the wall. "Which reminds me, I guess I should get going. I have some paperwork to deal with, and with Michael gone, we're little shorthanded. We were actually supposed to get an assistant deputy from the Highway Patrol to fill in for Michael, but he was delayed the first couple of days."

"I don't have any plans tonight, so if you want, we can go out for dinner or something?"

Jody nodded. "That would be great, or you could cook if you want? I know you make some amazing food."

"Klaus did insist on sending me to culinary school."

Jody nodded. "At least husband number-three was good for one thing."

Daphne laughed. "That, and his daughter Elle is still the sweetest thing. Did I tell you she's going to have a baby?"

Jody blinked. "How can she be old enough?"

"She's twenty-three."

Jody blinked as she realized how time had passed in that weird way it had of sometimes speeding up while feeling simultaneously slow. "She was eleven when you got married."

Daphne nodded. "And here she is, about to be a mother herself." She shuddered slightly. "I'm so glad I won't be expected to endure the title of grandma."

"You can always be a Gram like mine instead of a grandma."

"That's the only kind of grandma I'd ever consider being, but I'll still pass." Daphne glared at her. "Bite your tongue and go to work, woman."

With a laugh, Jody exited the kitchen, feeling better than she had since their semi-argument the night before. She still had her reservations, but if Daphne really slowed down and took time to get to know Ryland—while allowing Jody time to get to know him and more about him—she wouldn't be so concerned.

Daphne had a history of rushing in, and that normally was only putting her at risk for heartbreak. This time, it could mean her very life, and that still gave Jody pause, but she would have to defer to Daphne's judgment and keep her eyes open. With any luck, Ryland really was as special as Daphne thought, and maybe her friend could finally find happiness. It would certainly be the everlasting kind if she loved a vampire.

Chapter Six

Isabel

She felt ridiculous as she walked down the street to Valeria and Gertie's shared abode. It was a charming side street full of Victorian homes, though she wasn't certain if they were authentic, or if someone had just had a wild hair to imitate the style. They were certainly old, but she couldn't be sure of just how old. Regardless, all the homes were in good repair, and she imagined it would cost a pretty penny to live in the neighborhood. It was definitely pleasant, if a little bit old-lady and froufrou for her taste.

She double-checked the address on her phone to confirm she was at the right house, since she only vaguely remembered the exterior from her visit decades ago, and stared at the delightful pale-yellow home that could've been described as a gingerbread house were it smaller. It had a clapboard exterior with a gabled roof and hand-cut shingles, and was practically dripping in authenticity. It was exactly the sort of place she envisioned when she imagined ladies having tea.

With a sigh and a slight grumble under her breath at having been reduced to this, she adjusted the silly hat she'd purchased just that morning and flared her toes inside the sensible pumps she wore. Never having really been to tea before, she had envisioned wearing a stuffy suit, fancy hat, and pumps, and so she had dressed accordingly.

She tottered up the walkway to the house, and not because her knees were bothering her, though they were. The walkway was a little uneven, and it needed to be filled, lifted, or otherwise leveled in some fashion. She proceeded carefully, not wanting to break a hip and risk being caught in such an embarrassing getup.

She reached the porch seconds later and stepped up on the stairs. The third one creaked, but it seemed sturdy enough, and she proceeded onward. She rang the doorbell, and the door opened in seconds, with

Valeria on the other side. Her possibly new friend smiled at her, opening the door for her to enter. "You look lovely, Isabel."

"You looked just how I pictured," said Isabel, struggling to smile politely. Valeria wore a dove-gray suit edged with white, a string of pearls, and a matching pillbox hat with a cute little net that obscured part of her forehead. It seemed rather nauseating to go to all this pretense just to sit around and drink tea, but she reminded herself that Valeria was infinitely preferable to most of the other options for socializing available to her in Harrow Bay. She definitely didn't want to return to the Senior Center, and she had no plans to do so unless sheer loneliness drove her to desperation.

Even afternoon tea with a bunch of old ladies was better than that. She followed Valeria into the home, and the décor inside was just as precious and authentic as the outside, though updated from her memory.

It kind of looked like Laura Ashley had thrown up inside, but Isabel made the appropriate sounds of appreciation for the interior and found herself taking down the name of Valeria's interior designer as if she really cared, or as if she owned the house where she lived.

It was certainly a large house, and her knees ached a little bit as she followed Valeria down a long hallway before entering a sitting room. It was filled with delicate furniture, floral print wallpaper, and the requisite large tray of tea, cups, and a fragile-looking teapot right in the center.

There were other ladies in attendance, including Gertie. She appeared as absentminded as she had upon first meeting. Her polka dot hat sat askew on her head, and there was oatmeal on her matching polka dot suit, but it was obvious Valeria had made an effort, so Isabel went out of her way to greet Gertie. She took her hand and said, "How lovely to see you again. That is quite the outfit you have there, Gertie."

Valeria came up to her and smiled. "It was always one of Mother's favorites. Come and meet the others."

Isabel followed her around the room, meeting a couple of other ladies of similar age, and then finding a surprise. There was a woman with deep black skin and salt-and-pepper curled hair arranged in a natural style and pinned up underneath a snowy white hat, with elegant French tips on her fingernails.

Isabel wasn't at all surprised to find a black woman in their midst. What surprised her was that Monica Carlson had to be at least twenty years younger than the average age of attendees. She found herself seated beside the woman, soon learning Monica's brother owned one of the bars in town, and her nephew was a doctor at the hospital.

"Don't you feel a little out of place here?" Isabel asked after a few minutes of chitchat, as the other voices around the room covered what could possibly be a faux pas by asking.

Monica sent a knowing glance around before sipping her tea. "I suppose you're referring to the median age. Honestly, that doesn't bother me. These ladies are all part of the hospital auxiliary club, so they're dedicated to fundraising. That's my job."

"You work for the hospital?"

Monica shook her head. "Not work, but I volunteer. I'm so proud of what Scott does there, and it's a little hospital. We've only had it for fifteen years or so, and we're always struggling to make ends meet. Every lady here has done her part and more to ensure we have some funds. Anything that will get us away from accepting donations from the bloodsuckers is good enough for me."

Isabel blinked. "The bloodsuckers?"

Monica slanted her a glance. "I know you know about Harrow Bay. Anyone who pays attention knows what happened with you and Mrs. Gilling at the Senior Center."

Isabel choked on the Mexican wedding cake cookie she'd just put in her mouth and started to chew. She gulped it down with tea. "You, err, know about that, do you?"

"It's reasonably common knowledge, at least among those who want to acknowledge the truth." Monica lowered her voice conspiratorially. "My late husband was part demon, which is why we settled in Harrow Bay. He's been gone many years." It was difficult to tell from her pragmatic tone whether she was still bothered by that, or if she was just good at hiding her sadness.

Perhaps she'd just adapted, or maybe the marriage had been an unhappy one. Isabel could certainly relate to that, having been saddled with Andy for years, at least legally. The relationship itself hadn't even lasted a year before she walked out on his abusive ass, but it had been more complicated to get a divorce in those days, and it had taken her far too long.

"But what about the bloodsuckers?" asked Isabel.

"Ostensibly, it's a donation, but we all know there are strings attached."

Isabel frowned. "Bloodsuckers? Do you mean vampires? Someone told me bloodsucker is an offensive term."

Monica looked startled and then let out a hearty chuckle. "I guess it might be. Yes, I'm referring to the vampires, Ms. Campbell."

"Call me Isabel. So why are a bunch of vampires donating to the hospital? Aren't they immortal?"

Monica shrugged. "As far as I know, unless they happen to have an accident that parts their head from their body. I think a stake through the heart does it too. And I think maybe they naturally age, but slowly."

"I get the feeling you don't like them much."

Monica smiled. "How perceptive of you. I suppose I have no objection to them in general, and I'd prefer they get blood that's donated than take it from unwilling victims, but it still doesn't sit well with me that the hospital funnels part of our blood donations each year to the vampires in exchange for cash."

Isabel gasped.

"I'm pragmatic enough to understand the necessity, but that's why the ladies' auxiliary is so important to me. If we can find a way to replace the so-called donations from the vampires, we can end that distasteful arrangement. At least, I hope the board in charge of the hospital would be willing to, though Mrs. Tatum seems perfectly happy with it, and she heads up the board."

Isabel was fascinated, and a little put off too. "Do your donors know where the blood is ending up?"

Monica shook her head. "I can't imagine that would go over well, can you? So many humans living in Harrow Bay are in denial of what's around them. I have a feeling donations would dry up, which means funds would dry up as well."

"It's all sort of scandalous. Who would've guessed the hospital would have a deep and seedy underbelly?" Isabel sipped the tea, grimacing at the light floral taste. It was fine, but there was nothing particularly remarkable about it. She'd much prefer a glass of sherry or perhaps red wine. Even a slug of whiskey would've helped the bland beverage go down easier.

"Isn't that the way of Harrow Bay? Everything seems typical, serene, and practically perfect on the surface, but as soon as you look a little deeper, you realize the truth."

Isabel nodded. "I suppose that's correct. It's common knowledge then that the vampires are buying blood from the hospital?"

"I wouldn't necessarily say common knowledge, but it's certainly known among the finance team, the board, and the auxiliary to a certain extent. And of course, Ryland, since he's in charge of the vampires. I hold a seat on the board, but I'm more involved with the fundraising, which is how I know so much about it."

She lowered her voice slightly. "I don't suppose they're doing anything illegal, you understand? And when the donors give blood, they all consent for the blood to be donated to a specific experimental program, so they understand they aren't giving it in a life-saving capacity, at least not in the way they'd imagine. They're also compensated for it, so it's all as free of exploitation as it can be, but I just don't like the setup."

"I can't blame you. It is rather sordid."

After that, conversation settled, and the women started to focus on their next fundraising task. They decided to organize a local auction with donations from various businesses.

Isabel sat quietly, not really contributing anything. Tea wasn't all that exciting, but she imagined she'd come back if she were invited again, though that likely meant embracing the task of fundraising for the hospital. It wasn't Isabel's forte, and she suspected she might even have to be nice to people while maintaining a deft touch and light fingers as she picked their pockets after they willingly opened them.

She wasn't sure she could do that, even if it meant having a social outlet, but she could give it a try. It might even have the unexpected benefit of helping the hospital escape the seedy arrangement they had with the vampires to obtain human blood. Isabel shuddered as she thought of that, picturing vampires appearing at the back entrance of the hospital, passing over wadded bills as they waited for a baggie of blood that they ingested right there with ravenous abandon.

In her mind, it was rather like a drug den, though she had no experience with those either. She couldn't imagine there was much difference though, except vampires needed blood to survive, and addicts only felt like they needed their drug of choice to stay alive in most circumstances. Either way, she shared Monica's distaste for the arrangement and would be happy to help end it if she could.

Chapter Seven

Willa

She cursed softly when she saw lights in her rearview mirror. The car was too low to the ground to be Jody's SUV, so she assumed it must be Aoife's car, since she recalled her daughter mentioning Michael was on vacation for the week. Instead, a man she didn't recognize stepped out of the cruiser, and she realized it was from the state police rather than Harrow Bay.

She rolled down her window cautiously, feeling guilty though she had no reason to, at least not that she could recall. She didn't believe she'd broken any laws, but she was still tense as she waited for the officer to reach her.

He came to her window after what felt like an excessively slow saunter from his car to hers. He knelt slightly, and she realized he was around Jody's age. He was a little soft in the face and doughy in the middle, with a receding hairline, but he had a grin like a Lothario, and she was immediately on edge. Not because she felt guilty for anything or worried about a ticket, but for an entirely different reason. It was the leer he gave her.

"Hello, ma'am. Do you know why I pulled you over?"

Willa shook her head. "I can't imagine why."

He laughed in a knowing way, and it held an intimate tone that made her stomach curl slightly. "Of course, you don't, darlin'. I suppose you have no knowledge of the coasting stop you made there without fully stopping?"

Willa opened her mouth to protest, knowing she had come to a complete stop, but she realized that would mean spending more time with the man. He might even see it as an opening that she was offering a way out of her ticket. Instead, she gave him a tight smile. "I didn't realize."

"I might be inclined to let you go..."

"That won't be necessary, sir. If I broke the law, you should give me a ticket." She was brusque as she leaned forward, reaching into the glove compartment to retrieve her registration and insurance card. She passed it to him a moment later before getting out her driver's license and handing it over as well.

He frowned, looking irritated, but he quickly wrote down her information. She was surprised when he didn't go back to his car to verify it. Instead, he just handed her a ticket for three hundred dollars along with her items. She blinked at the amount. "Isn't that a lot for a rolling stop?"

"It's the penalty." He sounded as brusque as she had now, and he nodded, but he didn't really look at her. "Have a nice day, Mrs. Shaw."

She clenched her hands around the steering wheel, waiting until he walked back to his car before she exhaled and called him a very unkind word under her breath. She was almost embarrassed at the obscenity, but that didn't make it any less apt.

Talk about an unfair ticket. She was certain she hadn't failed to come to a complete stop, and even if she had, she was also positive it wasn't a three-hundred-dollar offense. She would definitely take it up with Jody, she decided, as she put the car back in gear and eased out onto the road after waiting for the state trooper to pull around her. He roared off with a squeal of his tires, indicating he was disdaining the speed limit. She didn't find that at all surprising, considering his whole manner.

Shaking slightly, she covered the rest of the distance to home and found the delicious smell of garlic and tomatoes filling the house when she entered. "Something smells delectable."

"Daphne's cooking for us," said Jody as she entered the living room from the kitchen, holding a glass of white wine for her mother.

Willa's mouth watered. "That sounds wonderful." She had barely finished speaking when her phone rang, and she retrieved it from her purse. "Hello?"

"Hi, it's Patty. I'm staring at my refrigerator, and nothing leaps out at me. I thought maybe you'd want to grab a bite to eat somewhere? Perhaps *Santiri's*?"

Willa hesitated, about to say yes, but then another whiff of Daphne's dish hit her nose. "Actually, I sort of have plans."

"Oh." Patty sounded so disappointed.

"Hang on just a second." She looked at Jody, who was still standing nearby. "Is there plenty if I invite Patty over for dinner?"

Jody nodded. "You know Daphne. She usually makes enough for leftovers...for a week."

"That way I don't have to cook so often," said Daphne from the kitchen with a laugh. Clearly, she'd heard the conversation, or at least part of it.

When Willa brought the phone back to her ear, she discovered Patty had heard as well.

"You're really inviting me over for dinner, Willa?"

"Of course. You can't miss my daughter's friend's cooking. Daphne has some amazing skills."

"It certainly sounds better than anything I could throw together, and if I leave now, I can slip out before Liesel gets home and guilts me into bringing her along or going out to dinner with her instead." Patty laughed lightly. "If she even bothers, of course."

"You'll be over soon then?" At Patty's confirmation, she quickly ended the call. She followed her daughter into the kitchen, taking a moment to glance at what was on the stove. She didn't quite recognize the cuisine, but it appeared to be Middle Eastern from the spice profiles and the vegetables she saw displayed neatly on the counter. "That smells delicious. It's not too spicy, is it?"

Daphne frowned. "You still don't like spice, Willa?"

She shrugged. "I can handle a little bit, but it's Mother's digestive tract I'm more worried about."

"It's worse than ever," said Jody with a small frown.

Daphne laughed, pushing back hair from her face. "It's a little spicy, but hopefully it won't cause Isabel's flatulence to flare."

"What's that about my flatulence?" Isabel entered the kitchen, looking like something out of a Norman Rockwell painting.

Willa's mouth dropped open in shock. "Mother, is that my suit?"

"It certainly is. I don't own anything this dull." She touched her head self-consciously, where a luxurious hat rested. It definitely wasn't her mother's style.

Willa moved closer. "What's gotten into you? Have you had a stroke?"

Isabel stuck out her tongue. "Ha ha. If you must know, I was invited to a ladies' tea, and I figured this would be the kind of getup one would wear to that. I was right. There were so many ridiculous hats, it could've been mistaken for Ascot."

Willa frowned. "Have you been to Ascot, Mother?"

Isabel waved a hand. "Of course not. Horseracing and England aren't really my thing, dear. I'm not a complete ignoramus though."

Willa had to bite her tongue, and she heard Jody and Daphne quickly stifling a snicker at her mother's antics. Trying to remain solemn, she said, "You really do look wonderful. Very ladylike, Mother."

Isabel scowled and immediately ripped the hat off her head. "That's the last thing I ever wanted to do."

Willa took the hat, rescuing it before it could fall to the floor. She fluffed the fake flowers and straightened the feather. "Shall I just put this in the top of your closet, so you have it for your next tea, Mother?"

Isabel grumbled, but she nodded. "I might just keep this suit too if you don't mind. It's too big, but it works with a tight belt."

Willa frowned. "By all means, you should keep it." Truthfully, it was a little tight across her hips, so she hadn't worn it in quite a while. Her mother was a few sizes smaller than she was, but she didn't have to make it sound like Willa's suit hung on her like a tent.

Feeling a little miffed, she took the hat upstairs and placed it in her mother's closet, willfully ignoring the stack of books she saw there all relating to how to unlock one's magical potential. The less she thought about her mother learning magic, the better she felt.

By the time she returned downstairs, the doorbell was ringing, and she moved forward to open it. She wasn't at all surprised to find Patty on the other side, and her friend held out a bottle of red wine.

"I wasn't sure what everybody was drinking, or what would go with your daughter's friend's meal, but you never come to someone's home empty-handed, right?"

"I think my mother loves this vintage." Willa groaned softly. "That means she'll probably drink more than one, and her already tenuous control of her tongue will be practically nonexistent."

Patty didn't seem all that sympathetic about the plight. "I'm sure she'll simply be more entertaining than usual."

Willa shook her head. "If you can call it that." From the way Patty laughed and followed her into the kitchen, she assumed Patty liked her mother's antics. Most people tended to get caught up in them, but Willa couldn't deny she was painfully embarrassed half the time when she was with her mother.

Isabel had no filter. Perhaps she'd had a moderate one when she was younger, but it had faded away over the years, and now she tended to say what was on her mind, no matter how inappropriate or insensitive. That certainly wasn't Willa's style.

They sat down after Jody relegated them to the table. Shortly after, Daphne brought over a tajine, along with a long, wide, shallow skillet filled with rice, spices, and vegetables. Once they had divvied out dinner and all had glasses of wine, conversation flowed surprisingly easily.

Willa was a little nervous and on edge, and she kept watching Patty's hands. She wondered if the other woman would reach out and touch her casually in a way that aroused suspicion, and it made her a little tense, at least until she let herself have another half-glass of wine, bringing her to two-and-a-half for the evening. That allowed her to relax slightly, at least until her mother went and ruined it all.

"He's just wonderful," said Daphne with a sigh and an enamored look. "I've been waiting to meet a man like him forever."

"Goodness knows you've certainly tried often enough," said Isabel.

Willa frowned at her. "Mother, must you be so rude?"

Daphne laughed, waving a hand, which caused her assortment of bracelets to jingle merrily. "Please, Willa, it's fine. I prefer Isabel's bluntness. It's not any secret that I have a horrible history with men. I think Ryland might change all that."

Willa frowned as her mother twitched slightly. "What is it, Mother? Are you all right?"

Isabel was frowning, and she swallowed more of her third glass of wine before answering. "I'm fine, but did you say Ryland?"

Daphne paused, looking at Isabel before nodding. "I did. He's who I've been talking about for the last ten minutes, Isabel."

Isabel frowned. "I didn't realize. You didn't say his name before, but I guess Jody mentioned it the other day."

Jody looked mildly interested, and Willa was bracing herself for her mother to say something terrible. "I don't think you even know him, Mother."

"I'm sure you don't, Gram," said Jody.

Isabel shrugged. "I might not know him, but I just heard his name again this afternoon."

Daphne frowned. "In what context?"

"It was at that ridiculous fundraising tea for the hospital when I learned the vampires have an arrangement with the hospital. They make generous donations, and in exchange, the hospital 'donates,'" She used finger quotes around the word, "Blood for experimental purposes. Of course, it's to keep the bloodsuckers alive."

Daphne looked startled for a moment, and Jody looked concerned. Then Daphne laughed. "That's a good one, Isabel. How long did it take you to come up with that?" She seemed to be admiring Isabel's wit.

Isabel frowned. "I'm not joking. That's what the woman from the board, and the head of the ladies' auxiliary, told me. Monica Carlson."

Jody looked unsettled. "Is she related to Scott Carlson?"

Isabel nodded. "I think so. I think she said that was her nephew's name. He's a doctor at the hospital."

Jody was really frowning now, and Daphne just looked bewildered. She shook her head. "Thank you for that information, Isabel."

Quickly, Daphne changed the subject, telling them about her visit to Dubai two years ago, and how she'd ridden camels through the desert and been forced to take shelter overnight when there'd been an unexpected sandstorm. Fortunately, her younger guide had found a way to keep her entertained, though he only spoke some English, and she'd spoken no Arabic at all.

Willa was embarrassed and unable to allow Daphne's story to distract her. She shot her mother a look. "Why must you always cause problems?"

Isabel looked defensive. "I don't know what you're talking about."

"You always have to push buttons and get a rise out of people. Can't you just let Daphne enjoy a blossoming romance without making up wild tales?"

Isabel scowled. "I'm not making up any tales. I'm simply telling you what I heard." With an annoyed huff, her mother pushed back from the table. "Thank you for a lovely dinner, Daphne, but I seem to be getting indigestion."

"That's too bad, Isabel. I hope your stomach feels better soon."

"I'm sure it will be less sour when I get away from certain people." Isabel shot Willa a pointed glare as she marched out of the room.

Willa startled slightly when Patty touched her thigh under the table. She glanced at her girlfriend, who was giving her a sympathetic look. Willa buried her face in her hands. "I don't know what gets into her sometimes with the things she says."

"Don't be hard on her," said Daphne before Patty or Jody could say anything. "I think it's part of aging. You start to lose some of your grip on reality."

Willa nodded slowly, starting to agree, but then a niggle of doubt hit her. She had dismissed her mother's claims about Sally Gilling for months, and her mother had been right all along. What if she was right about the vampires too?

Not that Willa wanted to admit such things existed, and she certainly didn't want to acknowledge that they might live in the same town as her, but after the truth about Sally had come out, she'd promised herself she would be more open-minded and listen to her mother more, without dismissing everything she said as her wild imagination.

That sent a chill through her, though she managed to smile, but it felt tight and stretched her lips in an uncomfortable fashion. Fortunately, conversation soon moved on from Ryland, Isabel's claims, and everything else that could be considered controversial. Instead, Daphne regaled them with further stories of her travels, and Willa pasted on a polite smile, aware of two things—the unnerving possibility that her mother was right about vampires, and the warmth of Patty's hand on her thigh.

She hadn't moved it, and Willa put her hand over Patty's discreetly. A shiver went through her, and she wasn't certain if it was anticipation or still fear about their planned night together. She was determined to see what happened and to see it through, but she was nervous. The thought of spending the night with Patty was almost as nerve-racking, albeit in a different way, as was the idea of sharing the town with vampires.

It was only closer to bedtime that she remembered to tell Jody about the ticket. Even then, her thoughts were mostly on Patty, and she forgot to listen to Jody's proposed solution. She just smiled and nodded, pretending like she had as she went into her room, feeling like a besotted fool.

73

Chapter Eight

Jody

Jody wanted to talk to Gram about her claims regarding Ryland, the vampires, and buying blood from the hospital, but Gram's door was shut when she woke early the next morning. Her grandmother wasn't downstairs when she got coffee and made herself a quick breakfast either, so she would have to wait until she was done with work for the day. As much as she wanted to dismiss Isabel's claims, they resonated with her and certainly had a ring of truth, at least for anyone who knew vampires lived in Harrow Bay.

She made it to the office around her usual time, so she settled in with her book to focus on practicing the spells and continuing to memorize some of the more complicated incantations. Even the slightest mispronunciation could result in a failed spell. She supposed it might even cause a major blunder or something potentially dangerous, so she was diligent about practicing the pronunciation. Though she didn't speak the language, the book included a clear pronunciation guide, and she felt like she was getting the hang of it.

Some of the spells were becoming so ingrained that she didn't even really have to think about them before they came to mind. She wasn't yet adept enough to just think the spells and have them work, but that was a rare talent among magic practitioners. Since she was in tune with the town's magic, there was a chance she might discover that skill and develop it further, but Jody wasn't counting on it. In case she had to always be able to verbally pronounce the spells, she intended to be prepared to do so.

She was engrossed in practicing when there was a knock on her door. Jody looked at the clock reflexively, realizing it was past nine. A good part of the morning had already passed her by, and she hadn't even had more than one cup of coffee. She cleared her throat and called, "Enter," as the door opened.

She was expecting Aoife, or perhaps Tara or maybe Beez, but not the soft-looking, average man who stood in the doorway. He wore a State Troopers uniform, and she realized he must be Bob Smith as he entered her office, holding out a paper. She took it and glanced briefly at the written confirmation that he was there to fill in for Michael. She nodded and put it on her desk. "You're late...by a whole day after calling to tell me you'd be late three days ago."

He shrugged. "Things happen sometimes, Sheriff." He winked at her in a suggestive way, and it was enough to make her skin crawl.

She frowned. "You could have maintained better communication. As it is, the week's almost over. I'm not really sure we need you now."

He frowned as he sat down in the chair across from her desk without waiting for permission or an invitation. He kicked back as though he were completely relaxed and had nothing better to do. "Don't be like that, Jody."

She scowled at him. "I think Sheriff Shaw and Deputy Smith works well enough, considering our short acquaintance."

He shook his head. "That's a real tragedy."

Intrigued in spite of herself, Jody arched a brow. "What's the real tragedy?" Had something horrible happened to him to prevent his scheduled arrival? If so, he sounded awfully cavalier about it.

"I just think it's tragic that women feel like they have to be hard-assed and overly aggressive just to prove they're strong enough to hold a job like yours."

Jody gritted her teeth together to keep from uttering her first response. She took a calming breath. "Excuse me?"

"I get it, darlin'. You feel like you need to maintain a tough exterior, or people won't take you seriously. It's okay to be soft and feminine though. You can be polite, even downright sweet, and still be taken seriously. I promise." He winked at her again, which seemed to undo everything he'd just assured her was possible.

Jody shook her head. "I don't know who you are, or who you think you are, but you have no right—"

With a weary sigh, he held up a hand. "Sorry. I shouldn't have said anything. Just an observation I've had over the years. Women like you feel like they need to overcompensate to prove they're just as good as a man. You sure are, but in a different way."

She dug her fingernails into her hands to keep from screaming at him. "You don't know me or anything about me, Deputy Smith."

He shrugged. "I might not know you personally, darlin', but I know your type."

She kept her voice level, though it cost a considerable amount of control. "You don't know anything about my type either. I'll tell you this now, Deputy Smith. If you call me darlin' one more time, we're going to find out if it's physically possible to wedge a foot in someone's ass."

His eyes widened, and he seemed temporarily taken aback. Then he chuckled. "My apologies, Sheriff Shaw." He still spoke in that same condescending way.

Jody decided it was a lost cause, and unless he became a blatant nuisance, she'd just let it go for now. That didn't mean she wouldn't mention his complete misogyny when she wrote up his report after he'd finished filling in for Michael for the rest of the week. She cleared her throat. "That reminds me. You gave my mother a ticket last night."

He frowned. "That knockout was your mother? How old was she when you were born, like five?"

Jody shook her head, but it wasn't to answer his question. It was in pure irritation. "I think you might've made an error on the amount you put down. Three hundred seems excessive for a rolling stop. That's more like a speeding violation of fifteen miles over the speeding limit."

He hesitated for a moment and then shrugged. "I might have written it wrong. I'll be sure to review it, Sheriff Shaw."

She nodded tightly. "Thank you." It cost her a lot to offer the meager words of gratitude, since she wasn't feeling anything like gratefulness toward the man. She could barely tolerate him, and she was looking forward to the week ending, with Michael returning to duty.

Fortunately, he left after that, and Jody was called out to address a few issues in the community. By the time she returned to the Sheriff's Station, it was nearly lunchtime, so she stopped by *Carroll's Grocery* and grabbed a prepackaged lunch to take back with her to the Sheriff's Station. As soon as she entered, she saw Tara and Aoife in a quiet conference with each other. Tara waved her over, and she went toward them. "What's up?"

"Ugh," said Tara with a sigh of disgust.

"Completely," said Aoife in an affirmative tone.

"Let me guess, the new deputy?" At their simultaneous nods, Jody found herself nodding as well. "Ugh just about sums it up, I'll agree. I thought men like him were practically extinct, or at least had enough sense to hide their Neanderthal side in the workplace. How the heck does he maintain a career with the state troopers while being such a misogynist?"

"I have no idea. If he calls me darlin' one more time..." Tara gnashed her teeth together with obvious frustration.

"Feel free to slap him," said Jody with a small laugh. "No, I don't suppose you should do that, but keep track of every incident. After all, I do get to file a report about his performance here once he's gone."

That made Tara grin, and she leaned back slightly in her chair with a nod of satisfaction. "I'll be sure to do that. I have a feeling the count will be in the hundreds by the time he leaves, and he's only here for the next couple of days."

"I can't wait for him to be gone."

Jody nodded her agreement at Aoife's statement. "I don't know why they sent him anyway. He was a day late, and he hasn't done anything yet besides give my mom a ticket that was way out of proportion for her supposed violation." Seeing Aoife's look of confusion, Jody quickly explained his traffic stop the night before he officially filled in for Michael. "Mom said he was kind of sleazy, though of course she didn't phrase it that way. I don't disagree at all."

The other two women nodded their agreement as well, and then Jody left to take lunch in her office.

When she entered, she found a surprise. Drake was at her desk, his boots propped up on the edge, and he had his arms angled back, with his hands folded together to cradle the back of his head for support. As soon as he saw her, he swung his long legs down and stood up, coming over to embrace her. Jody closed the door before kissing him, glad to have the blinds drawn. "I wasn't expecting you." She awkwardly held up her bag from Carroll's Grocery. "I just grabbed lunch for one."

He shrugged. "That's okay. I brought lunch for both of us."

Then the delicious smells hit her, and she realized he'd brought in *Curly's BBQ.* She breathed in deeply in appreciation. "If I didn't already have plans to keep you around, that might cement it." She set aside the prepackaged lunch, planning to put it in the refrigerator shared by everyone at the Sheriff's Station in a little while, but right now, the hot brisket beckoned, and she sat down in her chair, opening the Styrofoam container in front of her.

Drake had returned to his perch across from her desk, and he opened his at the same time. They both let out a satisfied sigh, and that was simply from the delicious smells that wafted toward them. "There is something magical about this barbecue." Jody dug her plastic fork into the pile of brisket.

"It could be that Curly's a kitchen witch, but I don't know for sure." Drake took a moment to douse his in Curly's special sauce, and they spent the next few minutes eating mostly in silence. It was the kind of meal that required full attention to savor and appreciate.

When Jody had eaten enough that she could finally put down the fork and focus more on conversation, she said, "I didn't know you'd be by."

"I like to surprise you. Besides, I had a little bit of time free."

She leaned forward slightly. "How did it go at the bar you went to last night?"

He huffed a sigh, and it was obvious it hadn't gone well. "If anybody knew anything about Honsiu, they wouldn't say. I can't imagine he has many friends, or anybody who'd be anxious to shield him, so when they told me they didn't know anything, I kinda have to believe them."

"I'm sorry that didn't pan out. What's your next step?" Before Jody could get an answer, there was a knock at her door. The knocker didn't wait for an invitation to enter, and the door swung open a second later.

Bob Smith sauntered in, holding a computer printout. He didn't glance at Drake to start with. Instead, his gaze was on Jody, and it had the same creepy edge of evaluation he'd displayed earlier. "Here you go, Sheriff. A gift from me to you." As he spoke, he tore the page in half theatrically before tearing it in half once more and tossing the fourths into the trash can.

She frowned. "What was that?"

"The incident report and the ticket for your mother. It's like it never happened." He wiped his hands together in a melodramatic fashion before tossing them in the air. "Poof, all gone."

Jody stared at him for a moment. "Thank you. I wasn't asking you to tear up the ticket, Deputy Smith. I just wanted you to reevaluate it for errors."

He winked at her. "Maybe I made a mistake giving her the ticket to start with."

She ignored the wink and the intimate tone as Drake let out a little growl in the back of his throat.

That finally got the deputy's attention, and he turned to Drake. He stiffened, and his displeasure was obvious. Drake was frowning at him severely as well, and she wondered for a moment if they were going to tear into each other seemingly without provocation.

After a second, Deputy Smith relaxed slightly and nodded his head. "Sorry. I didn't see you there, and I didn't know the sheriff had any visitors." He looked at Jody then. "Are you doubling as a parole officer, Sheriff Shaw?"

That elicited another growl from Drake, and Jody rolled her eyes. "Drake, this is Deputy Bob Smith. He's filling in for Michael for the next couple of days. He was supposed to be here earlier in the week, but things happened." Her tone was lightly mocking as she repeated Deputy Smith's words back for Drake.

Drake was frowning severely at him. "Yeah, I'm sure."

"Well, I just wanted to tell you about the ticket, and I thought maybe we could grab some lunch, but I see you're already eating, so I'll get back to work then. Thanks, dar...Sheriff Shaw." He amended his final parting as she gave him a death glare. With a nod of his head, the deputy left, closing the door a little harder than necessary, so that the glass pane in the door rattled slightly.

"Who is that?" There was still a growl in Drake's tone, and his eyes flashed red for a tick to indicate he was having difficulty controlling his anger. That was a bit worrisome, because he was more likely to let out the demon and drop his glamour when he was in a mood like that.

Not that Jody cared about seeing his demon side, but she didn't want Deputy Smith to stumble into her office on some other pretext and see Drake in mid-morph. "He's just some guy the state sent to us for the next few days. I imagine he gets shuffled around a lot because he's so annoying."

Drake frowned. "I didn't like the way he looked at you or talked to you."

"Neither do I, but I can handle it. I'm trying to ride it out and report it all when he leaves, but if I have to, I'll deal with it more firmly and decisively in the meantime."

Drake still seemed on edge for a second. "Are you sure you don't want me to talk to him?"

Jody quickly shook her head. "I don't think so. I appreciate you wanting to look after me, but it's really not necessary." She could just imagine how much further Deputy Smith's misogyny would be on display if he thought she needed her boyfriend to stand up for her. "It's fine. Really. Besides, I know you're busy trying to track down Honsiu. I have my things to focus on, and you have yours. Getting that demon back is far more important than putting some arrogant little jerk in his place, don't you think?"

He muttered something before leaning back. It was obvious he was making a conscious effort to relax. "Yeah, I guess. If it moves beyond verbal, or if he's doing something you can't handle, you will let me know, won't you? I mean, it's okay to ask for help."

"I know, and I will if I need it." It seemed to soothe him, and they spent the next few minutes engaged in more average conversation.

Before he left, Jody considered bringing up the topic of children. She hadn't really had a chance to talk to him since the conversation with Daphne, and she was curious about his stance. She hoped it wasn't something that would come between them, but when she opened her mouth to broach the subject, she decided it was bad timing. He had other things to focus on, and so did she.

A serious topic like his desire to have children, or lack thereof, needed her full focus and his as well. It shouldn't be squeezed into the last five minutes of a quick lunch break. She kept the questions to herself and followed him to her door. He kissed her thoroughly before opening the door, giving her a quick parting, and closing the door behind him.

Feeling silly and a little sentimental, Jody cracked the blinds on her office door to watch him go. It was only as he reached the doorway less than a minute later that she looked away, dismayed to see Bob was watching her through the slat. She quickly let go of the plastic blind, and it closed immediately, shielding her from Deputy Smith. Talk about creepy. The state troopers must really be scraping the bottom of the barrel with that one.

She was about to return to paperwork related to the morning calls, but before she could even reach her desk, there was a knock at the door. She braced herself for it to be Deputy Smith, and her tone was less than friendly when she said, "Come in."

Aoife stuck her head in, and she looked surprised. "Did you and Drake have a fight?"

Jody frowned. "No, why?"

"You usually sound much happier after he's visited. Right now, you seem a little grumpy."

"Drake wasn't the problem." She sharply angled her chin in the general direction of where she'd seen Deputy Smith lurking.

Aoife's dark eyes widened with comprehension, and she nodded her head. "Yeah, that would make me cranky too. I'm sorry to bother you, but there's been a call."

"What's up?"

Aoife looked serious. "Perry Driscoll found a dead body behind the pharmacy."

Jody frowned. "I don't suppose it's natural causes?"

"It didn't seem like it from the call."

With a sigh, Jody locked the magic book in her desk, returned her Smith & Wesson to her duty belt, and followed Aoife from the office.

Chapter Nine

Jody

It appeared word hadn't yet leaked out that there was a dead body behind the pharmacy, because she and Aoife were the only ones on the scene. There was no gathered crowd to gawk, and other than Perry Driscoll, who was shaking slightly when they spotted him around the corner, there was no one nearby.

The pharmacist looked ill, but Jody wanted to see the scene first, so she drove the SUV past him and parked farther down the alley. As she got out to investigate, Aoife went to the back of the SUV and took a roll of yellow tape to block the end of the alley to keep looky-loos from bothering them.

Jody moved closer, walking around the body of a man who appeared to be homeless. Harrow Bay didn't have quite the homeless problem several cities had, but they had their fair share of people passing through, though she couldn't say she'd seen this face before. With the blood covering it, along with matted blonde hair and a full beard, it was difficult to tell much about his face anyway. He seemed to be a sturdy man, probably in his mid-thirties, and though he was rough from living as a transient, he looked like he would've been difficult for the average person to take down.

She stopped her circuit around the body and paused, kneeling to get a closer look at the neck. The man's fate was obvious, because it was impossible to miss the two slash marks across his throat. They could've been done by any kind of blade that wasn't serrated, so that didn't help her narrow it down. She wondered if she might have to call in a Forensic Services Division team from Salem to handle this.

As she looked closer, Aoife's footsteps behind her alerted her to the arrival of the deputy. Aoife nodded to her as she knelt on the other side, and they both peered closer to look at the wounds on his neck.

"They look pretty neat."

Jody nodded at Aoife's observation. "They do, but they're not completely clean. They're a little ragged here and here." She took the pen from her pocket to indicate two jagged areas.

Aoife leaned closer before she made a small sound that indicated her discovery. "What is that?"

Jody shrugged her shoulders as she put her pen back in her pocket, careful not to make any contact with the body. "If I had to venture a guess, I might say teeth marks?" It was almost a question, but she was pretty confident. Whatever had happened to him, someone had made an effort to hide it by adding the slash marks to his throat, but they hadn't done as good a job of hiding the evidence as they'd thought.

"He seems pretty pale, don't you think?"

Jody examined his skin closer, seeing a tinge of blue around his mouth. His skin was alabaster, except for the parts marked with blood. He definitely had blood on his throat and chest, and there was even a little on his chin, but she thought there should've been more considering the nature of the injury. "Call the corner for me, if you would?" She hoped the coroner could give her a preliminary cause of death, though she was normally slow.

Aoife nodded her confirmation and was soon on the radio to Tara to call in the coroner. They stood together, backs facings the victim and looking out toward the alley, as they waited for Patience Horner, the coroner, to show up. Considering she also ran a funeral parlor in town, she could be in the middle of duties related to someone else's death, so it might be a while.

After a few minutes, Perry peered around the corner, looking uncertain. He took a step toward them, and then another before finding the courage to take a third.

"Do you think it's going to take him or Patience longer to get here?" Aoife asked from the corner of her mouth.

Jody cracked a smile. "I wouldn't want to bet money on either one." When he continued to hover, she gestured him forward with a sigh of impatience. He scuttled forward, though he hung back several feet from them, and even farther from the body.

"He's dead, isn't he?" Perry was sweating. He was a tall, spare man, with a sparse covering of hair across his head. He looked to be in his mid to late thirties, except for the bald spot and his rapidly receding hairline. That made it harder to guess his age. He had thin, almost skeletal fingers, and he folded them together in an anxious fashion as he cautiously peeked around Jody before diverting his gaze to Jody again. "I'm sure he's dead."

"Yes, he's passed. Do you know him, Mr. Driscoll?"

His eyes widened, and he quickly shook his head as though knowing the man would implicate him in a crime. "Me? Of course not. I don't associate with men like him."

"Those who're down on their luck?" Jody tried to keep the question neutral, but it set her teeth on edge to hear the judgmental tone in the pharmacist's voice.

He looked like he was sweating even harder now, and he took a deep breath. "I... That is... I had never really seen him before except for last night." He finished that with a burst of speed.

After a second, when neither Jody nor Aoife spoke, he continued. "He was loitering outside the pharmacy, and I just wanted to close up. He asked me for some money, and I declined. Then he asked if I could give him some Neosporin, because he had a bad cut on his leg. I told him I wasn't a charity, and I sent him on his way. I half-expected to find the place broken into this morning when I arrived, but there were no signs of mischief. I didn't discover him until I emptied the trash from last night, bringing it out here in the alley to throw in the dumpster. I have no idea how he got himself into the situation, but I had nothing to do with it."

"It's a guarantee he didn't slit his own throat and make most of his blood disappear," said Aoife with a severe frown.

Perry wiped his forehead on the sleeve of his white coat. "I didn't mean to imply he did. I'm just saying, I had nothing to do with it. You can't think I did, Sheriff Shaw?"

"I don't think you did, Mr. Driscoll." It was obvious from how shaken he was, in addition to the lack of blood anywhere on him. It was conceivable that he had murdered the homeless man before rushing home to change into fresh clothes and call the police, but it seemed completely dubious that had occurred. Whatever had happened to the man happened sometime between last night and this morning.

After a moment, Perry shifted from foot to foot. "I temporarily closed up the pharmacy, but since he was never inside, is it okay if I reopen for business? I have customers waiting for their medications. Poor Mrs. Tansey is going on day three without her hypertension medication, since her doctor is always so slow to call in refills, and the poor woman's too absentminded to call them in before she's almost out."

Jody frowned for a moment and then shook her head. "I'm sorry, but I can't risk people traipsing through the crime scene, and right now, it's still pretty low-key. You can open once Dr. Horner shows up to claim the body."

He muttered something, and it was obvious he was unhappy, but he didn't argue. Instead, he nodded to them and returned to his perch around the corner, disappearing from sight.

"He's full of compassion," said Aoife in a dry tone.

"Practically brimming over with it, at least for his paying customers." Before she could say anything else, a black van turned down the alleyway, and she'd recognize it as belonging to the coroner even if she hadn't seen the white letters against the black paint that identified it as the county coroner's vehicle.

Seconds later, Patience Horner parked the van in front of them, blocking the alley, which was probably a good thing. It prevented people from glancing down and seeing much of what was happening, at least until they loaded the body onto the gurney and into the van. She slid out of the vehicle, coming toward Jody with her hand extended. "It's good to put a face with a name, Sheriff Shaw."

Jody nodded. She held out her hand and shook Patience's hand. The woman had a firm, almost aggressive, grip and Jody figured what she'd heard about her was true—she was a retired Marine doctor who had settled in Harrow Bay a few years ago to take over the funeral parlor, and she had run for county coroner. Since she had been the only candidate, she'd won by a landslide and continued to hold the office unopposed each election.

She was probably ten years older than Jody, with a solid frame, thick but not fat, tall, and imposing. She had tight curls that clung to her head, though they seemed free of any product confining them. Perhaps they were just well-disciplined from a life of falling in that fashion. Jody had a feeling not much fell out of Patience's ability to control.

The coroner peered over Jody's shoulder, frowning slightly. "That's nasty. I'm afraid I can't get to him until next week though. Maybe even ten days or so."

Jody frowned. She might have to break protocol and possibly offend the corner. "I don't think we should wait that long to determine what happened to him."

Patience walked around her, kneeling closer to the body. "What's there to determine? His throat was slit. "

"I think there's more to it than that." Jody knelt beside the corner and showed her the areas that weren't consistent with the slash of a knife. "I think someone cut him to hide the true wound. I need to know what I'm dealing with sooner rather than later. If you can't help yet...?"

Patience nodded. "I understand, but there's only one of me, and cases tend to pile up. If I'm not doing the coroner and medical examiner duty, I have the funeral home to look after, and my volunteer work. Someone's always dying around here."

"Yeah, but I'm afraid this one might be something more than natural causes. Would you mind if I had Dr. Carlson look at the body? I just want him to confirm if there's something underneath the slash marks." What she wanted was him to confirm if it could be fang marks, or perhaps human teeth. She was careful not to step on Patience's toes, but she was determined to have an answer sooner than next week.

If Patient was bothered by what could be conceived as usurpation of her authority, it didn't show. She shrugged. "As long as Dr. Carlson doesn't mind, I have no objection. I can take the body to him, but I can't let it out of my presence. Will that work?"

"I'll give him a call, but it should be fine. Um, let's just keep this between us, if I can rely on your discretion, Dr. Horner?"

After a moment, the coroner nodded. "Sure, you can, and I do get it. I wish I could move faster, but I sure can't right now."

Jody shrugged. "I appreciate your flexibility."

"If it comes to the safety of the town, we all have to be reasonable, don't we? We can't always color inside the lines to get things done, and believe you me, that was one of the hardest lessons to learn about living in Harrow Bay after a life spent in the Marines."

Jody grinned. "I can imagine it was difficult to accept."

"Life's about adapting though. Okay, I'll take him over, and you can see what Dr. Carlson says."

"I do appreciate it. I'll owe you one, Dr. Horner."

Patience waved a large hand, as though it was negligible. She got to her feet again with a slight groan, and she moved to the back of the van. While she was busy retrieving a gurney and a body bag, Jody moved off to the side and found Scott's number in her contacts. She dialed him a moment later, and she was relieved when he answered on the third ring. "Dr. Carlson, this is Sheriff Shaw."

"I know. You came up on my caller ID. What can I do for you, Sheriff?"

"I have a favor to ask. It's a little unorthodox. Are you at the hospital?"

"Yeah, and I'm due to be on shift for another four hours. Do you need me to come to you after I'm off work?"

"No. I'll just bring the problem to you. Maybe you could meet us in the parking lot?"

She could practically hear him shrug. "Sure, I guess I can do that. What's this about?"

"Cause of death. I need one established, though it can't be officially yet, since Dr. Horner's too busy. I've a feeling we shouldn't wait a week or more to find out what's going on here."

He sounded concerned. "Text me when you arrive, and I'll meet you there. Go around the back of the hospital to the employee parking garage."

"Will do. Thank you, Dr. Carlson."

By the time Jody hung up, Dr. Horner and Aoife had loaded the body into the back of the van, and the coroner nodded to her as she got behind the wheel. After Patience drove off, Aoife came to her, frowning.

"What is it?" asked Jody.

"I'm just wondering why you didn't ask Dr. Horner to decide the cause of death?"

"I did, but she's too backed-up for a timely answer."

Aoife frowned. "I see. And she's all right with Scott taking a look?"

"For the safety of the town, she is. She's obviously busy, but she was ready to write it off as just a knife slash on cursory examination." She put up a hand quickly. "I'm not implying she's incompetent by any means. After all, she discovered what happened to Artie, but it took a long time. I don't have time to waste right now. I have a bad feeling about this, to be honest. I need to know what I'm dealing with as soon as possible, and Scott seems like the best way to establish that."

After a second, Aoife nodded. "It didn't seem to bother Dr. Horner, so I guess it doesn't matter. I just want to make sure we can all work together as we need to."

Jody recognized the subtle warning. She nodded quickly. "So do I. I definitely don't want to step on anyone's toes, but sometimes, there's no time for diplomacy." She moved to the SUV. "I have enough time to drop you off at the station if you want to start the report, and then I'll head over to the hospital."

Aoife nodded her agreement, and they completed the drive mostly in silence. Jody wondered if Aoife was still bothered by her stepping outside the typical protocols, but she didn't seem upset. She just seemed quiet, perhaps lost in thought, as she stared out the window of the SUV.

As they drove up to the Sheriff's Station, she parked near the door, leaving the engine running so Aoife could climb out. As her deputy started to do so, Jody said, "Wait."

Aoife paused and looked at her. "Yeah?"

"Make sure you don't put the part about Dr. Carlson in the report, okay?" At Aoife's nod, she said, "Are you okay?"

Aoife blinked, looking startled for a moment, and then she shrugged. "I'm fine. Or I will be. Thanks, Jody." She flashed a genuine smile, albeit a brief one, and closed the door behind her a moment later.

Jody circled around in the parking lot and took the street that would lead her to the hospital on the outskirts of Harrow Bay. She arrived a few minutes later, and it was easy enough to find the employee parking garage.

When she entered the garage, she drove around until she reached the third level, and there she found the coroner's van with the back doors open. She pulled up behind it, turned off the engine, and got out. As she got closer, she saw Dr. Carlson inside. She looked around for Dr. Horner, seeing her sitting in the front of the van. She greeted Dr. Carlson with a quick wave before walking over to the driver's side. Dr. Horner put down the window as she said, "Thanks again for doing this."

"No problem." Dr. Horner looked troubled. "I feel like I should apologize. I should've done this myself. Sometimes, I get overwhelmed by the job, and I don't always think to prioritize certain deaths over others."

Jody shook her head. "I'm the one who feels like I should apologize. I definitely stepped on your toes by requesting this consultation with Dr. Carlson."

"We all do what we have to. I promise I'll be more flexible in the future, Sheriff Shaw."

"I appreciate that, Dr. Horner, and if I step on your toes or stray into your territory, feel free to let me know." The older woman smiled and nodded, and Jody looked up as she heard Dr. Carlson exiting the van.

He circled around and walked toward them, holding a cloth. She could see bloody gloves wrapped in it as he paused in front of them, looking troubled. "His throat was cut, but I think it was done postmortem. There's no bleeding around the edges, and it looks like they were trying to hide the marks underneath."

Jody nodded her agreement. "What do you think those marks are?"

Scott's troubled look deepened. "If I had to guess, I might say fangs."

"Like from a vampire?" asked Jody as she observed Patience's reaction peripherally. The coroner stiffened a bit but didn't look shocked.

He hesitated again, but he slowly nodded. "Can't say with a hundred percent certainty, especially since the bite marks are mangled, but I definitely saw enough to identify what could be a couple of puncture marks. Vampires have four puncture marks, along with sometimes leaving an indent of their flat teeth, depending on how viciously they bite. There's not enough flesh to recover a good imprint to identify for certain, but I wouldn't rule it out."

Dr. Horner muttered something, and it sounded like a curse. Jody had the inclination to curse as well, and a chill went through her. "When do you think he died?"

"Maybe eight hours ago?" He shrugged. "It's a little harder to tell since I don't have all my instruments, and he was bled practically dry, but I guess around eight hours."

That definitely fit with the timeline the pharmacist had given her, sometime the night before or this morning. Certainly before early afternoon, when he'd discovered the body while taking out the trash. "I have one more question for you."

He nodded. "Anything I can do, Sheriff Shaw."

"Does the hospital have an arrangement with the vampires to buy human blood?"

He gulped audibly, and he looked disturbed. "Where did you hear that?"

"Let's just say a little bird told me." That wasn't entirely untruthful, because her grandmother had slightly resembled a bird with strange plumage in that ridiculous hat she had worn.

Scott looked nervous. "It's not something I'm allowed to discuss, Sheriff Shaw."

"In other words, you can't confirm it?" When he nodded, she said, "So you just did."

He blinked a couple of times, but he said nothing else besides, "Is there anything else I can do for you?"

Jody shook her head. "No, not this time. We'll leave it to Dr. Horner to handle the official results. Thanks for your time, Dr. Carlson."

He nodded and waved, heading back into the hospital without another word.

Jody turned the corner. "I guess there's no huge rush now, but if you find anything else significant when you get ready to look over the body, can you let me know? Not that I think this case will be ongoing in a week or more."

If vampires were targeting people in their town, she couldn't afford to wait a week to get confirmation. Having seen the feral vampire somewhat in action, though she hadn't seen the actual murder he'd committed, she could well imagine how a feral vampire could attack the town.

Still, she wasn't entirely convinced this was the work of a feral vampire. The one and only time she'd experienced one, he'd been out of his mind with hunger and animalistic rage. He certainly hadn't seemed to possess the necessary thinking skills to hide what he had done even poorly by slashing over bite marks to disguise them. This seemed the act of someone cool and calculating, who was trying to hide what they'd done, or at least obfuscate the investigation enough to make it complicated to determine who had done what and when.

She parted from Dr. Horner a moment later, returning to her SUV. There was one more task in front of her, and she was dreading it. She drove out of the hospital and turned back toward town, driving through to the other side, quickly finding the way to the Santiri compound.

It was as well-fortified as she remembered, and she had to wait for entry, but less than a half-hour later, she stood in the yard waiting for Ryland to join her. She was startled at the sight of Daphne stepping out onto the porch with him, and it made her uneasy. She glared at Ryland, though she tried to sound normal for Daphne. "I didn't know you were here."

"I'm just leaving. Ryland has to go as well in a minute. I was dropping off something to surprise him."

"She brought me crème brûlée." Ryland smiled at Daphne, and he seemed completely normal. Other than her own instincts, there was no indication he was anything but human.

"I need to speak with you, Mr. Santiri."

Daphne frowned, walking closer. "You sound so official, Jody," she teased. "You aren't here to warn him not to hurt me, are you?" She laughed, clearly delighted by the idea.

Jody gave her a tight smile. "I'm sure you can take care of yourself, Daph." Normally, that was true, but she wasn't entirely confident it was in this situation. It seemed more and more likely she was going to have to tell Daphne the truth about her new boyfriend, but she wasn't going to do it right now if she could help it. "It's something for the town."

Daphne nodded. "It sounds serious and very official, so I'll leave you to it." She paused long enough to kiss Ryland lightly on the cheek, and she waved her fingers at Jody as she walked past her, heading toward her rental car.

Neither Ryland nor Jody spoken until Daphne had gotten in the car and driven away, honking the horn twice as she left. As soon as her car had disappeared down the driveway, and Jody saw it enter the road a moment later, she whirled to face the vampire. "What's she doing here? You told me humans aren't allowed at the compound." Actually, it was Megan who had been the one to tell her that, come to think of it, and she'd only said humans didn't live at the compound.

He frowned. "I wasn't expecting her to drop by, but I couldn't just tell her to go away."

"So, she has no idea what you are?" Jody crossed her arms over her chest.

He hesitated. "No, not yet. I care about her a lot, and if we get serious, I'll definitely tell her."

"I think you should warn her before you get serious. It's a lot harder for her to walk away if she really cares about you before she discovers the truth."

He scowled. "You just assume she's going to walk away. I have a lot to offer Daphne."

Jody arched a brow. "Like what? Snacking on animal blood?"

He flinched, and he was frowning fiercely. "I'd take good care of her. I already care about her, and I can feel us getting closer. I take care of those I love. Besides, I can offer her something she desperately wants."

Jody sniffed. "What might that be?"

"She can look young for the rest of her life. I can offer her virtual immortality at the pace we age."

Jody's mouth dropped open, but she couldn't summon a counterpoint, because she realized he was right. As much as aging was bothering Daphne, her friend was likely to find that aspect of vampirism appealing. Would she be able to overlook the distasteful chore required to maintain her immortality and drink blood to do it? That, Jody couldn't be certain of, since Daphne was a little squeamish. The sight of blood often left her queasy, so it was difficult to imagine her friend summoning the fortitude to drink blood several times a week for the rest of her unnaturally long life if she was converted.

"I'm not going to hurt her, and we'll have a frank discussion soon."

She recognized the conciliatory tone, and she nodded once before shifting the conversation. "I'm not here about Daphne, but it is a serious topic. The pharmacist discovered a dead body behind the pharmacy this morning."

He flinched. "I'm sorry. That's always awful."

"It is, particularly when the body is about nine pints low on blood. Someone went to great pains to mar the teeth marks so it looks like his throat was slit. Someone bit the man, drained his blood, and tried to hide what they'd done." She couldn't keep the accusation from her tone.

His eyes widened, and then he looked angry. "It wasn't any of my people if that's what you're suggesting, Sheriff Shaw."

"How am I supposed to know that for sure, Ryland? Do you expect me to just take your word for it?"

He glared. "Actually, I do. People around here know I'm good for my word, and I don't say something if it's not true."

"If that's the case, why did you tell me none of you drink human blood?" Seeing him flinch, she said, "I know about your arrangement with the hospital. So, what's really going on here, Mr. Santiri? You're buying human blood while pretending you aren't. You told me your people were under control, but if they're drinking human blood, it doesn't seem like it will take much for them to get out of control."

He was so aloof that she was certain he wasn't going to answer, so it was a surprise when he said after a long pause, "It's true we have a certain arrangement with the hospital. It's not what you think. We have the peoples' consent, at least in a roundabout way, and we financially compensate the donors and the hospital."

"That's great, but it still doesn't explain why you lied to me."

He sighed, running a hand through his salt-and-pepper hair. "I didn't really lie, at least not technically. Most of the people here at the compound subsist on animal blood and regular food. Sometimes, particularly among new vampires, they have a hard time adjusting to the animal blood. We start them on human blood and gradually mix in the animal blood until they adapt. It's almost like how you would change your pets' food over."

Jody rubbed her eyebrows, trying to stave off a headache. "I see." She didn't know what else to say. It sounded like a plausible explanation, but it still indicated he had lied to her. "I don't know if I can trust you, Mr. Santiri."

He snorted. "It's not like you ever trusted me or my people, Sheriff Shaw."

That rankled, but there was an element of truth to it. "I'm sorry, but you put me on edge."

"I'm sure I do. It's the prey in you recognizing the predator."

She put her hand on her Smith & Wesson. "Are you threatening me?"

His eyes widened, and he looked alarmed. He even took a step back. "No, of course not. I'm just making an observation. The evolutionary instinct inside you recognizes me as a hunter. I have no intention of hunting you, and neither will my people. Whoever killed the man in town, it wasn't any of us."

Jody wanted to press for more, but without evidence, what could she do? "I expect you to talk to all your people. If you have even a hint of doubt that any of them are telling you the truth, or that they were involved with killing this man, I need to know. Otherwise, it means we have a rogue vampire on our hands, and I assume that means he or she isn't under your control."

He frowned. "I don't control the people who live here, Sheriff Shaw. I look out for them. I'm not some dictator or tyrant, but I do know what's going on, and I'm certain none of my people were involved."

"If it wasn't your people, then it means someone out there poses a risk to Harrow Bay, and neither one of us knows about it. Do you have some way to sense a vampire in your territory?"

He nodded. "I do. I'll make a circuit around downtown later tonight, and I'll focus particularly on the pharmacy to see if I can get any hint of another vampire's presence. By now, their pheromones have probably faded to nothing, unless they're still around, but I'll check it out."

"I appreciate that." Her words were stiff, and she still hadn't completely discounted his people as the source of the problems. Perhaps Ryland himself was as together as he seemed to be, and maybe he wasn't the one drinking human blood, but he'd still hidden the truth from her, and that meant some of his people weren't quite as in control as he claimed.

It left her nervous and would have done so even if they hadn't discovered a body drained of blood. Under those circumstances, and considering he was dating her best friend, her anxiety was bordering on outright hostility with a strong dose of fear. "If I find out you're lying to me, and you're hiding the person who killed the man we found, they'll go down, and so will you. I'll make sure you're close to Sally Gilling in one of the special prisons located around here. Are we clear, Mr. Santiri?"

"Crystal." The word dripped with ice.

She nodded to him and turned away, though the hairs on the back of her neck stood up. It went against her nature to turn her back on him, but she refused to show weakness by backing away and keeping her eyes on him at all times. She made sure her senses were open and alert, but he didn't bother her, and neither did any of the other vampires living at the compound as she returned to her vehicle.

When she was in the SUV, she locked the doors, though she didn't think that gave her much more than the illusion of safety. She doubted glass and steel would be any major deterrent to any of the vampires who might want to get through the vehicle and tear out her throat. The thought made her shiver, and she was glad to turn on the engine and feel a blast of heat filling the cab a moment later. She was several miles away from the Santiri compound before the chill dissipated, and she felt close to calm again.

Chapter Ten

Willa

Willa had been quietly stewing about the forthcoming sleepover with Patty, so when she arrived at her house that night, her palms were sweaty, her stomach was twisted in knots, and she was certain she wouldn't be able to say a single thing. Patty would open the door, invite her to come inside, and Willa would just stand there frozen on the doorstep, completely paralyzed from fear. She might end up spending the rest of her life trapped in that position.

Even being aware it was a ridiculous fear, she couldn't deny it haunted her as she slowly lifted a hand and rang the doorbell. There was an element of excitement, but mostly, she was just frightened of what was coming. She was certain she was going to let down Patty in every way that mattered, and she found it difficult to swallow past the lump in her throat as the doorbell rang.

It only took Patty seconds to answer, and Willa drew in a deep breath as her girlfriend opened the door and pushed open the screen door to invite her inside. She was so nervous she barely noticed the neatly arranged house, and she was only vaguely aware of walking down the hallway behind Patty, who led her into the kitchen.

"I thought we could start with dinner." As Patty spoke, she nodded her head toward the table that was already set. There were large glasses of a deep red wine, a mixed salad in a wooden bowl, and what looked like homemade pizza resting on a stone.

Willa swallowed again, managing to utter a sound this time. "It looks lovely. You didn't need to go to all this trouble. We could've just ordered takeout."

Patty waved a hand, which caused the neck on her oversized sweatshirt to slide slightly down her shoulder, revealing the delicateness of her collarbone. Willa stared at it for a moment, her mouth dry for a different reason.

"No, I like cooking. I don't always feel like it, but when I do, I want to go all out."

Willa smiled as she followed Patty to the table. "I admit, it's a nice change to have someone cook for me."

Patty passed her the bowl of salad. "Your mother and daughter don't cook?"

Willa couldn't suppress a slight shudder. "It's not that they don't so much as they probably shouldn't." She let out a small laugh. "Jody has reasonable skills, and my mother's actually not terrible, but she likes to put spice in everything. You know, she once made oatmeal laced with chocolate chilies? I had no idea what they were. I thought they were raisons until the first bite."

Patty laughed, covering her mouth with her hand as she did so. It took her a moment, and then she quirked a brow. "You're certain Isabel didn't do that just to get to you, dear?"

"The thought crossed my mind, but she ended up eating the entire pot by herself in two mornings. Let me tell you, Jody and I were both relieved when the last of that horrible dish was gone."

Patty served her a slice of pizza as she nodded. "I've definitely heard of the horrors of your mother's digestive tract."

"I don't think it's because she's getting older either. It's always been that way with her. I can remember even as a little girl I'd feel dread every time Mother cooked something spicy. At least she didn't insist on making everything for me spicy as well."

"You aren't able to handle the heat?" Patty asked in teasing voice as she stroked her fingers across Willa's hand in a suggestive way.

Willa laughed, feeling a little awkward, and she quickly diverted the conversation to something else. They spent the rest of the meal talking about pleasant topics that didn't have any true depth. Willa hoped she was doing a good job hiding her nervousness, but she almost jumped out of her skin when Patty stood up and grabbed the wine bottle and her glass. "Let's go to the living room."

Willa nodded, swallowing the lump in her throat again as she lifted her half-full wineglass. She was somewhat feeling the effects, and she knew Patty must've been generous with keeping it topped up throughout the meal. She appreciated the extra lubrication that made her more relaxed, though she was still exceedingly tense. She was certain she was hiding it though as she sat on the couch by Patty, at least until she jumped slightly when Patty brushed her arm.

Patty chuckled as she put down her wineglass and the bottle on the coffee table. "Relax, Willa. I'm not going to pounce on you. If nothing happens, that's absolutely fine."

Willa nodded, embarrassed that she hadn't hidden her nerves very well. She leaned forward to put her glass on the coffee table as well, and when she leaned back, Patty put an arm around her shoulders. That didn't make her stiffen with surprise. Instead, she focused on relaxing and curled against her as Patty lifted the remote. After a quick debate, they decided on a rom-com they had both seen before, so it didn't require much attention.

Willa and Patty watched it sporadically for the next two hours as their caresses and kisses increased, moving at a gradual pace that Willa could handle. As the hours ticked past, she tried to remain relaxed. When Patty yawned for the third time, Willa said, "We should probably get to sleep."

Patty nodded. "Are you staying over? I'd like you to, but don't feel pressured to. If you do, it can be something as simple as just cuddling while we sleep."

Willow licked her lips and nodded slowly. "I'm sure I'm being ridiculous, but I'm not ready to rush into anything else yet. However, the idea of falling asleep in your arms appeals to me."

Patty grasped her hand as they stood up, and she led her down the hall to her bedroom. "It appeals to me too, Willa. Not everything is about sex, and I'm content to take our time."

Willa leaned forward and kissed Patty on the lips, holding her extra tight for a moment before easing back. "I appreciate that, Patty."

"I feel like we have all the time in the world."

Willa nodded, but she couldn't help thinking of Artie at that moment. Her mother's poor boyfriend had been downed by Sally Gilling, certainly not in the prime of his life, but a few years sooner than he probably would've gone otherwise. Life was unpredictable, and while she wasn't ready to rush into anything, she also decided she didn't want to move at a snail's pace either.

With that in mind, she helped Patty undress, and then Patty undressed her, and the two of them laid together in the bed. She turned out the light, and she reached for her girlfriend, enjoying the feel of her body against hers.

It was different compared to how it had felt to cuddle with Elton, but it was no less pleasant. In fact, she appreciated that it was different, because she knew she was different than she'd been before becoming widowed. When Willa had been Elton's wife she never could've imagined being another woman's girlfriend back then, so it was appropriate that things felt different with her.

***

Willa had brought her own car, but she followed Patty into the shop the next day, feeling closer than ever to Patty. They hadn't had sex, but they'd done what she would label some petting. It wasn't the physical aspects so much as the emotional connection that she was still ruminating on as they got to work.

She couldn't help feeling closer to Patty, and she thought Patty's connection to her was deeper than ever. She wondered how it would be if and when they reached the point where they became lovers in every sense of the word, and for the first time since contemplating it, she viewed it with more excitement and anticipation than nervousness or a sense of doom that it would end everything.

She wasn't paying much attention as she went outside to straighten the sidewalk displays. It wasn't until she felt a sensation like someone was staring at her that she stiffened and turned slightly. Willa grimaced as she saw Deputy Smith standing a few feet away from her. She nodded to him. "How can I help you?"

"I saw you out here puttering around, and I wanted to let you know I took care of your ticket, Mrs. Shaw." He winked at her in a nauseating fashion. "It wouldn't do to get on the sheriff's bad side by giving you a ticket, I suppose."

Willa bit her lip for a moment, uncertain how to handle it. Finally, she uttered a stiff, "Thank you." It felt wrong to thank him for tearing up a ticket he never should have given her to start with, but she wanted to be as civil as possible, especially since Jody had to work with him for at least the next couple of days before Michael's vacation ended.

He came closer, and his nostrils flared. "You smell different today."

She blinked and stared at him. "What?"

He shrugged a shoulder. "You smell different. You had a flowery kind of perfume before. It was quite intoxicating. It's not unpleasant by any means, but it smells like something else now." His eyes narrowed slightly as Patty stepped out of the shop then, and his nostrils flared again. "Ah."

Willa didn't like his knowing tone or the wink he sent her way. "Did you need something else, Deputy Smith?"

It was a perfect opening for him to gracefully exit, but of course, the man didn't seem to have the ability to be gracious. Instead, he shrugged. "I could use a new paintbrush."

"You're an artist?" asked Patty, sounding as friendly as she did with any customer. She had no idea who he was though.

He chuckled. "I work in unusual mediums, but I consider myself somewhat of an artist."

Patty frowned slightly, obviously finding his response as strange as Willa did. "Let me show you where the paintbrushes are."

As much as Willa wanted to wait outside and avoid the deputy, she didn't want to leave him alone with Patty, or her girlfriend at his mercy. With a deep breath, she followed them into the store, finding a surprising sight. Deputy Smith stood in the middle of the store, a strange expression on his face. His nostrils had flared again, and he looked at Patty and then Willa. "You had a ghost in here."

Patty blinked. "What? I'm sorry?"

He tapped the side of his nose. "It's a special sense I have. I don't get to use it much, but I can definitely tell there was a ghost here. Malevolent, right?"

Slowly, Patty nodded. "You're not from Harrow Bay."

He shook his head, looking surprised. "I'm not. Why?"

Patty shrugged after a moment. "It's just most sensitive people live in town, at least from my experience."

"You need to expand your horizons, ma'am," he said with a wink. He looked at Willa then. "You too, darlin'. Why don't the two of you travel? Then you could do whatever you wanted without having to reveal the truth to anyone."

Willa gasped. "I don't know what you're talking about, but I don't like your tone."

He laughed as though she amused him. "It's obvious you don't like me guessing that you smell like your friend here. It's all in the nose." He tapped the side of his nose again, which was quite large for his face. "You seem almost uncomfortable with the idea, to be honest. I'll be sure not to slip up and mention it to the sheriff. I'm assuming she doesn't know, right?" He winked at her.

Willa straightened her shoulders. "I don't think we have what you're looking for in the store, sir. You should move along now."

His eyes widened, and he looked like he might argue for a moment, but instead, he let out a low laugh. "That's okay. Your secret is safe with me." He winked at her and Patty before sauntering out.

Willa watched him go, resisting the urge to follow behind him and lock the door. She shook her head as she looked at Patty. "How does a man like that keep a job working for the police?"

"I don't know. He's pretty insufferable, isn't he?"

Willa nodded as she turned blindly to a display, making sure it was neat, though it had already been so.

"He's not entirely wrong though, is he?"

Willa stiffened at the slight note of injury in Patty's tone. She turned her head to look at her. "What?"

"It's pretty obvious you don't want anyone to know about us. Even that guy could tell."

"I don't want that guy to know anything about me. He's creepy, even if he is a cop."

Patty nodded. "I don't disagree, but even creepy perverts can be right sometimes. You'd be awfully embarrassed if he went and told Jody about us, wouldn't you?" She sounded neutral as she asked the question, but her eyes flashed, telling a different story.

Willa took a deep breath, struggling to find a good answer that wouldn't anger Patty but would be truthful. "I'm not ready to announce it to anyone else yet, but I'm not ashamed of you. I invited you over for dinner to spend more time with Jody and my mother so you would have a chance to get to know them."

Patty nodded, but she still seemed troubled.

"Have you told Liesel, Suzanne, or Miranda yet?" Willa asked the question with a slight air of challenge.

After a moment, Patty blinked and then shook her head. "I haven't. Liesel's the only one who lives close enough to be involved in my life on a day-to-day basis, and she's opinionated and bossy. She's not likely to take it well. Is that why you don't want to tell Jody? Do you think she's going to reject us?"

"No, not at all. My daughter's pretty open-minded. Much more than me, to be honest." She gave Patty a small smile, and it felt weak around the edges. "I just want more time for you and me to figure out who we are together before we announce it to everyone. I'm not embarrassed."

Patty frowned as she came out from behind the counter and walked over to Willa. She put her hands on her shoulders and squeezed lightly. "I sincerely hope not, because there's nothing to be ashamed of, is there?"

Willa quickly shook her head. "Not a thing."

"In that case, I guess there's no reason to announce it to our daughters just yet."

Willa nodded her agreement, quickly kissing Patty on the cheek before pulling back and going outside to finish straightening the outside display. In one way, she felt like she'd dodged a bullet, but in another, she knew it was a harbinger of an issue that might arise between them in the future if and when Patty was ready to announce the relationship, but Willa wasn't quite there yet. She didn't want to look for trouble or anticipate things that might keep them apart, but she couldn't help being a little worried about their timing not being in sync.

Chapter Eleven

Isabel

Isabel had just put in the tray of hot wings when the phone rang. She hurried over to answer. "This is Isabel."

"Isabel, it's Valeria Clements." Her new friend sounded distraught.

Isabel frowned. "What's wrong?"

"Nothing, at least nothing major, but the sitter who was supposed to come over and take care of my mom so I could come to your place for a few hours isn't going to make it after all. She's had car trouble or something." Valeria's voice lowered slightly. "I think she just doesn't want to deal with Mother. It's hard to keep a sitter."

"Is that all? Why don't you just bring your mother with you?"

Valeria hesitated for a moment. "Are you sure? Most of the time, she's in her own little world, but when she's lucid, she can be unpredictable."

"Is she going to stab us with a butcher knife, or take out her teeth and try to bite me with them?"

Valeria laughed softly. "Neither one is very likely."

"So maybe she'll drool a little, and maybe she'll pee her pants. Sounds like any other day at the Senior Center."

Valeria's laugh deepened. "Yes, I guess it does. Honestly, she'll probably just sit there the whole time and stare at the wall. She's lost in her memories, I think, when she does that." She still sounded uncertain. "Are you sure you don't mind me bringing her? She might interrupt our games of *Boggle*."

"It's not the end of the world if she does." She was certain Valeria was somewhat stir-crazy and ready to get out of her house, and Isabel was dying for some socialization, so she had no problem with Valeria bringing her mother along. After assuring Valeria of that once more, she hung up the phone and returned to preparing for her guests.

She added a third glass for some ginger ale she found in the fridge, figuring Gertie wasn't one to drink wine, particularly in the afternoons. She wondered if she should make a pot of oatmeal, but she thought that might be a cliché. She would wait to take her cues from Valeria when they arrived. If Valeria indicated the woman couldn't eat sausage and cheese like she had on the charcuterie board, and that the hot wings would be too much for her, she would find something bland to give the older woman. They had some saltines somewhere, didn't they?

It didn't take Valeria long to arrive. Isabel heard the van pull into the driveway. She hurried out to open the door and step onto the porch, holding the screen door open as Valeria casually used a stubby finger to lift her mother's wheelchair up the steps. She was clearly using magic, since she hadn't touched the chair, but it hovered slightly for a moment before it touched onto the wood.

Isabel nodded, appreciating that her new friend had some magical powers as well, and she was hoping she might be able to get her help on learning more. Isabel was still seeing Hersch, but she'd lost some of her drive with Sally Gilling's downfall, though she hadn't lost her interest in learning as much magic as she could. It just didn't seem as crucial to learn it all so quickly and reach a level of proficiency that could take on Sally.

Not to mention, she'd had a dose of reality when she'd faced Sally Gilling in the Senior Center. The woman could've basically broken her, or at least directed her minions to do so. Isabel had been aware at that moment just how little magic she actually possessed, and how poorly she commanded it.

In some ways, it had demotivated her to learn more, and she realized that abruptly. No wonder she hadn't been back to see Hersch more than once or twice since the Senior Center incident. It was something to dissect when she didn't have company, to decide if she wanted to keep learning magic, or if she was going to let it fall by the wayside as she had once as a young woman when she hadn't displayed particularly spectacular talent.

By the time her thoughts had cleared enough to realize she was still standing on the porch with the door open, Valeria and Gertie had entered the house. She stepped through, cleared her throat, and let the screen door close behind her before she closed the main door. She led them through the living room and into the kitchen, where the *Boggle* board was set up, along with the snacks lining one side of the table. "Is this okay for your mother, or does she need something else?"

"She can't really eat anything like that, but I brought her some pudding and *Ensure*." Valeria gestured to a bag hanging from the back of Gertie's scooter.

"Does she need anything before we start playing?"

Valeria shook her head. "No, she's calm and entertaining herself."

Isabel directed a glance at Gertie, who was looking avidly at an old copper pot hanging from the wall. Willa had received it as a wedding present years ago from a distant relative, though Isabel couldn't recall whom now. It might've even been someone from Elton's side. Even though she'd given up cooking in copper long ago after learning how unhealthy it was, she kept the pot and used it as a decorative touch in the kitchens where they'd lived.

It seemed to be quite fascinating to Gertie, so Isabel left her to explore the depths of it with her gaze and turned to Valeria. Soon enough, they were hunting words in *Boggle,* and Isabel hated to acknowledge it, but she was grateful for her glasses. It made it so much easier to pick out the letters—not that she'd confess that to her know-it-all daughter. She wasn't about to give Willa the satisfaction.

Several hours seemed to pass in the blink of an eye, and Isabel realized it was getting close to dinnertime. Gertie had made a soft sound, and her stomach gurgled, and that got both their attention.

"Goodness, she must be hungry. We should go so you can have dinner."

Isabel waved a hand. "Please stay for dinner. You can help me cook. It's not a chore I typically enjoy, and since your mom's hungry, we might as well feed her and not make her wait until you get home, right?"

After a moment, Valeria nodded her agreement. "Are you certain we won't be a bother?"

"Of course not. It's not going to be anything grand, but I think we have enough to make spaghetti and meatballs for everyone."

"My mother loves meatballs, though I'll have to smash them to unrecognizable bits." As Valeria spoke, she reached into the bag hanging from Gertie's chair, fishing out a bowl of pudding. It was in a genuine Tupperware container, in the nineteen-seventies avocado-green shade. She opened the lid and started feeding her mother.

Isabel stood up, grateful she wasn't in a position where Jody or Willa had to do such a thing for her, and she hoped she never got that feeble. With any luck, she would just drop dead someday from a catastrophic stroke or something else that didn't make her suffer too much ahead of time and didn't leave her withered and turning into a true old lady.

She moved to the stove and began cooking. Valeria joined her a short time later. Her new friend was boiling the pasta when they heard the front door open, along with the sound of voices.

"Back here," called Isabel, thinking she recognized Daphne's voice. There was a male voice as well, but she wasn't certain to whom it belonged. She wasn't entirely surprised to be introduced to Ryland the vampire less than a minute later, though Daphne didn't include that descriptor.

"Are you eating with us?" She looked at Ryland in a meaningful way. "I put lots of garlic in my spaghetti sauce."

He seemed amused, and when he smiled, she was certain his canines were a little bit longer than average. "I wish I could. I love the flavor, but it causes me problems."

"I can imagine." She sniffed.

"It used to be a favorite of mine when I lived in Rome many years ago."

Her eyes narrowed. "Maybe you have trouble because it's an anticoagulant? You'd hate to bleed out all that expensive blood."

He shrugged again. "It would take a massive amount to cause me such issues, Ms. Campbell, but any garlic does leave me feeling off."

Daphne rolled her eyes, clearly impatient with the conversation. "Honestly, Ryland, you don't have to indulge her." She looked at Isabel, shaking her head lightly. "I don't know what's gotten into you, Isabel, but I told him you thought he was a vampire. At least he's amused by it."

Isabel grunted. "Are you staying for supper?" she asked again.

"No. Thank you for the invitation, but I just came by to change. We're going to drive into Salem and have something a little fancier. Not that I don't adore your spaghetti and meatballs."

"I put in extra chili powder," said Isabel with a wink. She saw Valeria flinch slightly, and she hoped she hadn't made a mistake with her new friend's digestive system.

"Murderer."

Everybody froze, and it took Isabel a moment to realize from where the word had originated. She stared at Gertie, mouth open in shock, as the older woman surged from her scooter, standing on shaky legs and pointing at Ryland. "You murdered her. Murderer. Burn in Hell."

Ryland's eyes widened, and he looked unsettled.

"I'm so sorry," said Valeria. "She's old and gets confused."

Ryland cleared his throat. "It's fine, miss."

Daphne frowned. "You know what, I don't think I need to change after all. Let's just go, hon. Maybe we can get something at your place."

Ryland nodded his agreement, and they quickly left with a rushed parting, both ignoring Gertie's repeated accusations that he was a murderer. It took Valeria several moments to sooth Gertie while Isabel watched the whole scene unfold with a mix of confusion and fascination. According to Valeria, Gertie was often confused, but she couldn't help thinking there had been true depths of awareness in her gaze and conviction in her tone when she assured them all Ryland was a murderer.

Chapter Twelve

Jody

"Hey, Jody, do you have a sec?"

Jody turned from her office door, which she was closing behind her. "I was just heading out. What is it, Beez?"

"You know how I've been converting the microfiche to digital?"

She nodded. "I appreciate that—"

He waved a hand to interrupt her. "I'm not looking for thanks. I came across something you probably need to see."

Jody followed him as he turned around without another word and went back to the back room. She was right behind him, and she waited as he clambered up into the computer chair, using his overly long arms to provide better leverage to seat himself, and then he brought up a picture of an old newspaper article. "This caught my attention when I was extracting and converting, because I vaguely remembered hearing about it."

Jody leaned over his shoulder, peering at the computer as she read the article about a young local woman who'd been found with her throat cut. According to the story, Nila Dinwiddie had been murdered. It was a sad story, but she couldn't imagine its relevance, especially since it had happened eighty-one years ago.

"What did I need to see?"

"That was just the first article." He tapped a key on the keyboard, and the next picture he'd taken from the old microfiche came up, announcing there had been an arrest. Ryan Santiri, local butcher, had been implicated in the crime. There was a picture of him on the front page, and though it was black and white, she gasped, easily recognizing Ryland. She supposed she might be able to dismiss it as his father or grandfather's picture, but she was certain she was looking at a previous iteration of Ryland Santiri.

She leaned a little closer, wanting to read the smaller print. It announced Ryan had been arrested and was being held at the county jail under suspicion of killing his girlfriend, whose body had been discovered by her roommate, Gertrude Wilson. She skimmed that article, but it didn't tell her much. She looked at Beez. "Is there anything else?"

"More along the same lines covering the trial, but here's the interesting part." He clicked the key, and a new image appeared. It was announcing exoneration of Ryan Santiri due to lack of evidence. Beside Ryan's mug shot, there was a picture of the victim. The first one she'd seen of Nila hadn't been very clear, but this one certainly was.

It must have been a staged photograph, whereas the first one used had been grainy and slightly out of focus, thus obscuring the startling resemblance between Nila and Daphne. The paper had probably quickly acquired the first photo they could to print the scoop, but by the time the reporter wrote this one, they'd received a much better picture. She gasped softly. "Can you print me a copy of that?" At Beez's nod, she added, "Actually, all three of the main articles that tell the progression."

"Sure thing. I figured you might be interested, since the vampire was involved with this, and your friend's with him now."

Jody nodded. "What do you think the odds are that Ryan Santiri is Ryland Santiri?"

"Pretty good. He's lived here for at least a couple of centuries. He re-does his identity every generation or so, but it's him. He always smells the same."

"Thanks for the information, Beez. It's almost enough to give you a raise."

He looked intrigued. "You aren't paying me."

"Exactly, so add twenty percent." He gave her a disgruntled look, and she squeezed his arm in a thankful fashion as he passed her the pages. "Seriously, I owe you for this."

"You know what they say about making deals with demons. I'll be sure to collect." He called that after her with an evil chuckle as she rushed from the back room.

Jody didn't take time to respond, though she didn't feel the least bit afraid about making deals with Beez, whose power she'd seen the extent of on more than one occasion. Besides that, it certainly hadn't been any sort of devil deal.

She rushed to her SUV and headed straight home, even blowing through a red light and using the siren. She knew Daphne had plans with Ryland again this evening, and she was hoping to catch her friend before she left to meet him, or he picked her up.

She rushed into the house moments after Beez's revelation, calling, "Daphne?"

Gram appeared in the doorway to the kitchen. "She's not here. She took off with that Ryland character after Gertie said he was a murderer."

Jody skidded to a halt, blinking. "I... What? Who's Gertie?"

"Come and meet her."

Jody crossed the distance between them, and Isabel put her arm through hers. "You remember I went for the ladies' tea?"

Jody nodded, certain it had something to do with the situation, though she couldn't be absolutely certain her grandmother wouldn't go off on a tangent.

"Valeria was my hostess. I met her at the Senior Center, where she sometimes takes her mother."

"How old is Valeria?"

"She's seventy-six. We went to high school together."

"Her mother must be ancient." Jody winced as she said that, realizing how insensitive it sounded. "I mean, she must be quite old."

"I'm a hundred and two," announced a voice that sounded a little thready.

Jody's gaze darted directly to the source. She saw a small woman sitting in a wheelchair. She looked bright-eyed and alert, and she also seemed anxious. "You must be Gertie." She frowned then, still grasping the papers in her hand that she had taken from the passenger seat when she got out. "You wouldn't happen to be Gertrude Wilson, would you?"

Gertrude blinked for a moment, and then she smiled. "I used to be before I got married to Laurence Clements. Do I know you, dear?"

"She's not really all there," said a woman about Isabel's age, hovering near her mother's chair. She could only be Valeria.

"I'm having a lucid moment." She sounded acerbic as she gave that assurance to her daughter before looking at Jody. "How do you know me and my maiden name?"

"I saw it in an article." Jody hesitantly held it out, not wanting the woman to lose her grasp of reality since her daughter seemed to think she had a tenuous hold already. "It's an old article about your friend's murder." She gave that warning before Gertrude took the paper with a surprisingly steady hand.

The old woman looked at it for a long moment and then sighed. She handed it back to Jody and nodded. "I was the one who found her. We used to work together at the old canning factory outside of town. We canned crab all the time. That was back in the heyday, before all these regulations came in and cut out our jobs and shut down the factory." She sounded bitter, but she also seemed aware of the difference between then and now.

"What happened to Nila?"

"She was dating Ryan Santiri. He was the local butcher. I have to tell you, I never approved." Gertie shivered. "There was just something about him that was unnerving."

Jody nodded along, completely understanding. Perhaps the would-be prey in Gertie had responded to the predator she sensed in Ryland. "I saw he was exonerated."

"There just wasn't enough evidence to convince the jury, but you don't have to convince me. He slashed her throat and made a right mess of it, he did."

"I'm sorry about your friend." Jody kept her tone level, not wanting to upset the old woman. "Do you remember anything else about the event?"

Gertie hesitated and then shrugged. "That Ryan left for a few years, and then his brother Remington came to town. Ryan never came back. Running away sure seems like an admission of guilt to me."

Jody nodded, though to be fair, leaving could be a manifestation of wanting to get out of a small town that thought you were a murderer if you were innocent. She stood up fully and turned to Gram. "I have to find Daphne."

"They were going to go to some fancy restaurant, but she didn't take time to change. She mentioned something about his place. You might find them at *Santiri's*."

Jody nodded as she left her house less than a minute later, climbing into the SUV. She was on her way to *Santiri's* when her cellphone rang, and she directed it through the car's system to answer. "This is Sheriff Shaw."

"Hey, Jody, it's me."

She sighed in relief at the sound of Drake's voice. "Are you around?"

"No, I'm not. I'm a couple hundred miles to the south. I had a lead that didn't pan out, but I learned from a source that Honsiu probably wasn't strong enough to leave Hell with his full power. That means he might not be as formidable if I do find him."

"That's good to know." She struggled to hide her disappointment, wishing Drake were available to join her. "Will you be back tonight?"

"Yeah, I'm heading back now. Evita will take good care of me."

"See that she does," she said a little tartly. "I don't want you smeared all over the highway, so don't rush."

He hesitated. "Are you okay?"

She hesitated, struggling to sound normal. "I'm fine. Why?" She didn't want him to pick up on her distress and rush back, risking his safety in the process.

"I don't know. You sound a little off."

"I'm okay. I just have a case on my mind."

"I can understand. Do you want me to stop by tonight?"

"I would love that, and I don't care how late it is."

Drake chuckled softly. "I'm looking forward to it then. Bye, Jody."

"Bye." She pressed the button to disconnect the call, pushing down her disappointment. Part of her would've liked to have Drake and his demon magic at her side if she had to face off with the vampires, but he wasn't a deputy or her official sidekick. She was hired to handle situations like this, and she knew she could do it. She just wished Daphne weren't caught in the middle.

When she reached the restaurant, she parked in a no-parking spot by the front door and rushed in, interrupting the hostess, who was just about to seat a large group of people. "Is Ryland here?"

The young woman looked like she might protest for a minute, but then her gaze dropped to Jody's badge before lifting again, and she shook her head. "He took tonight off, Sheriff Shaw."

"Do you have any idea where he is?"

"He's at the compound. He called one of the busboys to bring home dinner for him and a friend, since their original plans were scuttled."

Jody nodded, already heading back to the door. "Thanks." She didn't bother to wait for any further response as she pushed back through the people, ignoring the way they muttered and glared at her, and rushed outside again. She'd left the SUV running, so all she had to do was climb inside, and she was off in seconds.

The few minutes to drive outside of town and reach the Santiri compound felt like forever, but she was finally going down the long driveway after gaining admittance through the steel gate. When she parked her SUV warily near the front door, she left on the headlights, though it wasn't completely dark yet. It was just starting to edge toward twilight, but she wanted as much light as possible. She didn't want them to take her by surprise.

When she stepped out, she wasn't surprised to find Ryland exiting the main house. Daphne trailed behind him, looking surprised and a little concerned. Daphne passed around him. "Is everything okay?" She looked worried. "It's not your grandmother or your mother, is it?"

Jody shook her head. "They're fine."

"Is it that batty old lady who called Ryland a murderer? Did she send you here?" Daphne sounded defensive then.

"She didn't have to, though she confirmed what I already knew." Jody held out the article about Nila's murder, trying to get Daphne to look at it.

Daphne glanced down, but she didn't really read it. "What's that?"

"Eighty-one years ago, your vampire boyfriend killed his then-girlfriend, and he got away with it."

Daphne's gaze widened, and she laughed. "What is this?" She looked around, as though searching for a camera. "Are you trying to trick me on some kind of show?"

Jody sighed. "That's not my style, and you know it. Look, I guess I should tell you a little bit more about Harrow Bay before I try to explain what's going on with Ryland."

He stood silently, and it surprised her that he hadn't offered any commentary yet. His arms were crossed over his chest, and he looked defensive as well.

Daphne was frowning severely now. She must be taking this seriously, because she didn't usually frown if she could help it, wanting to avoid wrinkles. "What are you doing here, Jody?"

She ignored that question. "This town is different than anything you've ever seen, Daphne. There's a Hell gate in the center of town, and it has its own magic, and there are creatures living here that you wouldn't begin to understand until you've seen them—"

"Like vampires?" Daphne's voice was full of scorn. "I don't know what's up with you, or why you want to sabotage the best thing that's happened to me in a long time, but it's really unfair. I've always been supportive of you. Why aren't you doing the same for me, Jody?"

"I'm trying to. I didn't want to tell you any of this, but you have the right to know. You're dating a vampire, and he has a history of killing people."

"I didn't kill Nila," said Ryland in a soft voice.

"Of course, you didn't," said Daphne. "You weren't even alive eighty-one years ago." She shook her head. "I don't know if your eccentric grandmother is rubbing off on you or what, but this is crazy, Jody. You need to get some help."

"I don't need help. I'm not the one dating a vampire." Frustrated, Jody shoved the papers into Daphne's hands, making her take them and not letting go until she had. "At least look at the evidence."

"Fine, sure." Daphne still held them in her hand, but she turned away from Jody. "When you're ready to talk about this without the craziness, you know where I am." With that, she strode back into the compound.

The hairs on the back of Jody's neck raised as she realized Ryland still stood there. She put her hand on her Smith & Wesson as she turned to face him.

He looked where her hand rested. "That won't help," he said softly.

"I'm aware silver might only slow you down, but don't worry, it's not my only weapon."

"I wasn't threatening you, Sheriff Shaw. I'm saying I'm not going to hurt you. I didn't hurt Nila either. I loved her, and I was going to marry her."

Jody snorted. "I love ham sandwiches, but I don't usually regard them as romantic partners."

He rolled his clear eyes. "You know it's much more complicated than that. Humans aren't just a food source, and I was feeding on animal blood and had been for a long time by the time I met Nila. Why do you think I ran the butcher shop before I sold it to the Divine family?"

Jody hesitated and then nodded, conceding that made sense. "Gertie identified you."

"She certainly didn't identify me from leaving the scene. I hadn't even been to their home for the past few days before Nila was murdered." He closed his eyes, looking pained. "I was trying to protect her, you see?"

Jody shrugged. "No, I don't see. How?"

"I had an enemy for a while. He was a vampire, like me, and it was an ongoing feud. I won't bore you with the details, but he cropped up every time he found me to stir up trouble. He observed me with Nila and realized how happy I was, so he went after her. He drank her blood and then slashed her throat to hide the marks. Gertrude found her, and the cops had no good explanation for why most of her blood was gone, and apparently, they didn't notice the teeth marks, or they chose to ignore them. Whatever the reason, they decided I was the most likely candidate, since she and I had been romantically involved."

"I only skimmed the articles, but you didn't seem to offer any good defense."

He shrugged. "I didn't really need to. I was working late that night, they had no proof tying me to the event, and they were forced to let me go after a short trial. I'm sure they all knew I wasn't guilty, but they had to blame someone. It's not like I could tell them Renard murdered her, could I?"

Jody's eyes widened, and she considered what he was claiming. "So, a vampire killed her, but it wasn't you?"

He shook his head. "Not at all. I understand if you don't believe me, Sheriff Shaw, but it's the truth."

"What about the resemblance between Nila and Daphne?"

He cringed lightly. "I really did love Nila, and I'll admit, that was the first thing I noticed about Daphne. She looks quite a bit like Nila, but she's nothing like her in spirit or personality. Please understand that doesn't make me like her any less. In fact, I think I could fall in love with her."

"You owe her the truth before you let her fall in love with you." Jody felt a smidgen of guilt as she said that, because she owed her the truth as well. She should've tried to explain the incredibleness of Harrow Bay and warn Daphne she was dating a vampire when the relationship first began.

"I plan to do just that. In fact, I'm going to right now, unless you want to try to talk to her again?"

Jody shook her head. "There's no point. Until you confirm what I've told her, she'll cling to the stubborn theory that I'm either crazy or out to hurt her for some reason. She'll never believe it on her own or on my word. Have her call me when she's ready to talk, okay?"

Ryland nodded, waiting until Jody had turned and gotten in her SUV. When she had the doors closed, he turned and walked back inside to the main house, and Jody spun around to go down the driveway, passing through the gates a moment later.

She wasn't entirely certain she could believe Ryland, but he seemed sincere. She realized she'd forgotten to ask what had happened with Renard, and it seemed like it might be important, in case the vampire still had an old enemy out there stalking him. Even if Ryland hadn't killed Nila, it didn't mean Daphne was necessarily out of danger just yet. The danger might come from someone unexpected though.

Chapter Thirteen

Jody

Jody decided to go by the station instead of heading home yet, since she would be closer to the compound if and when Daphne called. It was likely to be an experience that shook her friend when she learned the truth, even if she responded positively to Ryland being a vampire.

It probably wouldn't bother Daphne too much though. She was always one to look past problems and focus on her heart, and it was leading her toward Ryland. Maybe that would be a good thing for her friend, but Daphne wasn't always good about being rational and making sure she was doing the right thing for herself.

That was where Jody came in, and she decided she would keep an eye on the situation for Daphne. She only hoped Daphne would get over her anger and confusion and come to Jody, or ask her to come to the compound, so they could talk. She hated having this friction between them. It was like a hole inside her, and she knew only working it out with Daphne would make her feel whole again.

As she pulled into the station, she brought her phone to her ear after dialing Drake's number. She got the voicemail, so she figured he and Evita were on the road. "Hey, I stopped by the Sheriff's Station instead of going home. There's something I want to look into. If I leave here before I hear from you, I'll let you know that I'm heading home. Otherwise, come to the station first. Bye."

After hanging up and dropping the phone in her pocket, she slid out of the car and locked the SUV behind her. Jody entered the station a few minutes later, going into the back room. Beez wasn't in sight, and she wondered if he was out somewhere doing something, or if he'd just taken to a nook or cranny in the station, perhaps wanting to check on one of his social media accounts.

She went to the microfiche machine, finding a slew of articles from the time period of when Nila had been killed. She spent the next hour reading about the case, and as she got to the end of it, she concluded the jury had probably made the right decision. Several articles had pointed out there wasn't enough evidence against him, and two of his employees had seen Ryan Santiri working late the night Nila had been killed. The timing between their departure and Gertie finding her body was nebulous at best.

He would've had to pull off murder and blood drainage at extreme speed, and his attorney had focused on that. There was also an account of someone who'd seen a shadowy figure leaving the apartment area shortly after when the doctor had concluded Nila must have been murdered. He hadn't matched Ryland's physical description or body size, and it had been another point the attorney used to weaken the case against Ryan.

With a sigh, she leaned back and rubbed her eyes after turning off the microfiche machine. It seemed impossible to doubt Ryland's account after reading through everything. She wished she had the police reports from back then, but that would be difficult, if not impossible, to obtain, at least without a lot of digging. Most likely, they had all been destroyed years ago, or at least put in storage. She briefly considered the idea of looking through the microfiche files to see if the police records had been archived in such a fashion too, but she decided against it.

Jody pushed back from the office chair Beez was using for his project and stood up, stretching to work out the kinks in her back. Maybe she would pay him back for all his hard work with an ergonomic chair he could adjust. Or maybe it was already adjusted to his comfort level, since he was shaped quite differently from her.

She shook her head, realizing she was trying to avoid thinking about the topic at hand. She'd basically driven out and accused Ryland of murder without enough evidence, and she'd pissed off her best friend in the process. She only hoped Daphne could get past her anger enough to talk to her, but the only way she'd do that was if she accepted—

"Jody?" called Daphne as the main door rattled and slammed shut.

Jody hurried out of the back room, finding Daphne standing in front of the door that she had left unlocked. Her friend looked frightened, and her eyes were wide. Daphne held a handkerchief to her neck, and it was stained red around the beige cream. "What happened to you? Are you all right?"

"Oh, I did something so stupid." Daphne burst into tears as she threw herself into Jody's arms. Jody hugged her for a moment, patting her back and murmuring soothing words until Daphne finally calmed down enough to speak clearly. "I asked him to turn me. I believed him after he showed me what he really is, and I realized I would never have to get old, and he and I could be happy together. I told him I wanted to be like him."

"So you asked for this?" At Daphne's nod, a wave of relief swept through her. If Ryland had made this move on his own without her consent, Jody would've had to deal with him decisively. "Thank goodness."

"What do you mean? I think it was a stupid thing. I realized halfway through that I wasn't sure I wanted to do it after all, so I pushed him away, and I ran." Her friend swayed slightly then, and Jody brought her over to sit in Tara's chair, abruptly realizing Olly hadn't reported for duty, and he hadn't called in. She hadn't even noticed since she'd been preoccupied with seeing the microfiche files.

"Do you think it's too late to change my mind?"

Jody carefully eased away the fabric from the wound on her neck. It wasn't as serious as she'd thought, and the blood had slowed mostly to a trickle. There was definitely blood staining the handkerchief, but she wondered if it would've been so obvious on something that wasn't such a light color. "I don't think so. I know he carries some kind of enzyme. You didn't drink his blood, did you?"

Daphne's nose curled. "Of course not."

"I think that's a crucial step," said Jody.

"I didn't realize that. He just told me I'd have to drink animal blood."

Jody nodded. "Most of them, at least the Santiri people, do. A lot of the regular vampires out in the world consider humans a snack. I'm glad you're taking time to think this through."

"I think I rushed in too quickly. I really like him, but—"

There was a rattling sound from the storeroom, and Jody looked up. She expected to see Beez, but it was Bob Smith who came flying out of the room. She frowned in shock. "What are you doing in the storeroom this late at night?"

He didn't even look at her. Instead, he was focused on Daphne. There was a predatory look in his eyes, and his lips had skinned back from his teeth in a way that made Jody uneasy. "Deputy Smith, what are you doing?"

"Blood." He was practically salivating. He completely ignored Jody, shoving her aside as he rushed to grab Daphne and pull her into his arms.

Jody was frozen for just a second, trying to absorb what was happening. In that moment, Deputy Smith's face looked like it opened up, his jaw loosened, and a spiked tongue shot from his mouth. It was aiming for the wounds already existing on Daphne's neck, and Jody reached for her gun without thought. It was all instinct as she brought it up and shot Bob Smith through the tongue.

He let out a howl of agony, and it kept him from connecting with Daphne's neck as he turned to face her. He was holding his gaping appendage, and blood oozed from it. It should've been bleeding more freely, and she wondered how much blood was actually in his body.

She stared in horror as more of whatever was inside Bob started to emerge, apparently using his mouth as casually as someone would a revolving door. She let out a horrified gasp as a red, leathery-skinned *thing* started to slither out of Bob. The deputy dropped to the floor, moaning incoherent, but she didn't spare a glance toward him.

Jody was too busy watching the thing slithering her way as it freed itself from Bob. The more that escaped Bob, the longer it seemed to be. She wondered how it had stuffed itself inside him, and it was grotesque. As she watched, the tongue started to regenerate, and though it was shorter than it had been, the spikes were rapidly returning.

She brought up her Smith & Wesson again, this time aiming for the thing's face. She fired a round through what should've been its brain, and it shuddered for a moment, but it kept coming. It was like it absorbed the impact of the bullet, and the slug certainly didn't pass through.

Jody's hands were shaking, but she put the gun into her holster and started mentally flipping through her catalog of magic. She cast a binding spell, and bands of energy wrapped around him. He slithered and fought against it, and he had so many twisting appendages that he managed to free a couple.

One got loose and smacked Jody across the face, making her fly backward into Michael's desk. Her head was fuzzy, and her ears were ringing, but she forced herself to stand up as quickly as she could. The thing was still coming. It hadn't shaken off the binding spell, but it wasn't completely incapacitated either.

Jody uttered another incantation, hoping she had it just right, as she summoned a freezing spell. At first, it had no visible effect, but then the thing's tail started to turn blue and stopped moving. The ice slowly spread upward, but he was still coming toward her. Relentlessly, the creature approached her, reaching her feet and then her legs. She was still unsteady, and it knocked her down and slithered on top of her even as the ice continued to spread up its body.

Jody could feel the icy touch of its cold limbs against her legs, and she shuddered as she tried to push it away from her. Either it was too strong or too solid from the ice quickly consuming it, or it had its own magic, because it seemed to subdue her easily. She found her arms pinned to her sides as it wrapped one of its appendages around her, and the tongue stroked down her face. It wasn't in a sexual way at all. It made her think it was tasting her, and she let out a gagging sound.

"Hey," shouted Daphne.

Jody managed to turn her gaze just in time to see Daphne bring down the steel wastebasket and smash the creature on the head with it.

Unfortunately, that didn't do much to dissuade it. All it did was hiss at Daphne before turning back to Jody. The tongue was on her neck now, and she was certain it was going to pierce her skin at any moment. She couldn't help but macabrely wonder how long it would take the thing to drain her. Would it be over in seconds, or would it take a few minutes? Would it still be hungry when it was done with her and go after Daphne?

It was unnervingly quiet. The thing didn't say a word or make any sound at all. She imagined that might change to slurping sounds at any moment, and she strained to escape again.

"Leave her alone," said Daphne. She sounded like she was near tears.

Jody wanted to tell her to run, but she couldn't move. Where the thing had licked her, her face was numb, making her wonder if it secreted poison, or if it was just an anesthesia. Either way, her lips weren't moving, though she tried. She wasn't certain Daphne could outrun the thing anyway, but she wished her friend had the sense to try instead of standing around waiting for it to drain Jody and then go after her.

Not that she didn't appreciate the loyalty, and she would've done the same thing. She had more training than Daphne though. Unfortunately, she wasn't able to do nonverbal magic yet, so the spells she had memorized weren't going to benefit her.

The door crashed open then, and she heard the tinkle of glass followed by what sounded like more crunching under boots. Someone was rushing toward them. Someone sturdy and tall, and when she looked up, she saw he was angry and lethal. She'd never been so happy to see Drake, and if her lips hadn't been numb, she would've smiled at him.

With a roar, he ripped the creature straight from her, picking it up and hurling it onto the floor. Enough of it had frozen that it shattered into several pieces, and finally the creature let out another sound. It was similar to the one of agony it had voiced before, when she'd shot it through the tongue, but it didn't cease.

Drake marched over to it and punched it in the face a few times until it was quiet. As she watched, he opened a duffel bag and stuffed the remnants of the creature inside, closed it, and muttered an incantation.

Her lips were starting to move, and by the time he returned to her, lifting her into his arms, she was able to slightly kiss him back when he kissed her.

He pulled back slightly. "Are you all right?"

She nodded, trying to move her lips to form words. They weren't that cooperative yet.

He frowned. "Did he get some of his saliva on you?"

Jody nodded.

"It's a paralytic. He tends to use it on his victims before feasting on their blood while they're still alive."

Jody recalled Bob Smith then, but she looked at Daphne first to assure herself her friend was okay. Daphne looked unsteady, but she didn't seem injured other than the wound at her neck that was scabbing over.

Then she lifted a hand and pointed to the fallen deputy. Abruptly, she realized the dislike she'd had for him had likely come from whatever was inside him. He probably wasn't a misogynistic pervert. "What?" The word came out stuttering, and it was difficult to understand, but Drake seemed to grasp what she was asking.

"That's Honsiu. He has a meeting with Luc as soon as I get him back to Hell. He was a high-level demon before, but he won't be now."

Drake's control slipped, and his face flickered for a moment, revealing his red eyes and a hint of the demon inside.

Daphne gasped and took a step back, and Jody realized she'd seen the transformation. That meant she would have to tell her friend what Drake was too. Maybe it wouldn't matter, because Daphne would forget when she left Harrow Bay, and it seemed like she probably would be off again once her love affair with Ryland was settled.

"This deputy guy is lucky he was a host instead of a meal." Drake gently set her down in a chair before moving over to Deputy Smith, who was still out cold. "He's going to remember most of this, and he'll probably have some horrible nightmares about having that thing squirming around in his insides, but I think he'll survive. The host typically does."

"I wonder why he picked him?" asked Daphne.

Jody smiled at her with her eyes, since it was exactly the question she was thinking.

"It was probably an opportunity. He recognized a symbol of authority and figured he would bear less scrutiny if he were using the deputy as his conveyance."

Jody shuttered, thinking how many times she had been in proximity to the demon throughout the week without realizing it. She'd thought Deputy Smith was just disgusting. She hadn't realized he was being possessed by a demon.

"Should we do something for him?" asked Daphne.

Drake shrugged. "Nah, I think he'll be okay. He's probably a little bruised on the inside, but he shouldn't have any internal bleeding." He sounded sympathetic. "His jaw's going to hurt like a bitch though. He might need to go to the emergency room for realignment."

Jody nodded. "Probably. I swear his jaw unhinged with a cracking sound when that thing climbed out." The words were still slightly slurred and a little incoherent, but she sounded better, and she had much more movement than she'd had just a few minutes ago.

Drake smiled at her, coming closer and putting his arm around her shoulders. "I was so scared when I walked in and saw that thing all over you." He pulled her against him, lifting her out of the chair again and into his arms.

Jody hugged him back, enjoying the feel of his comforting presence. "Thank you."

"It was just pure luck I arrived when I did. I had no idea he was here. Everything suggested he'd moved away from Harrow Bay as quickly as possible, but maybe Luc's barrier magic was stronger than we all anticipated. Or the unauthorized trip out of Hell drained him worse than we thought. Since Luke isn't around to ask, I have to guess."

She frowned. "You said Luc wanted to meet with him when you get back to Hell though."

Drake looked at the bag, which was starting to squirm. "Great, he's regenerating. I guess he's thawed out now."

Jody shuddered again. "He can come back from that?"

"He's a demon. They're pretty resilient." Drake winked at her, though he didn't seem to really be in a lighthearted mood. "I signaled Luc as soon as I saw the thing and had him in the bag."

Jody was certain she hadn't seen any sort of radio communication equipment or other device, so it must be some way that demons communicated. She decided not to probe, not liking the idea of her boyfriend having a mental link to the devil. It certainly wasn't through his choice, so she couldn't dwell on it.

"I guess I should get him to Hell. Will you be okay for a little while? If not, Luc can just wait."

Jody shook her head. "I'll be fine. I don't think it's a good idea to make him wait. You don't want him to turn his anger at Honsiu on you."

Drake hesitated and his jaw clenched. "I'm willing to risk it if you need me."

"Daphne and I will make sure we get home safely. We can look after each other. But come see me whenever you get done. I don't care how late, okay?"

He frowned and then nodded. "It'll take a while in Hell, but time can pass differently there. I should be able to arrange it where I come back to you within a couple of hours." He sighed as he walked over to pick up the duffel bag. "I'd rather stay here with you than have to deal with this."

"No offense, but I'd rather you leave since you have that as your parting gift." Jody gave him a small smile, realizing her voice was barely slurred now. "The sooner he's back in Hell, the happier we'll all be."

He nodded in agreement before coming back to press a kiss to her forehead. He would've gotten closer, but Jody moved away from him. Not Drake, of course, but the unhappy package he carried in the duffel bag.

Daphne waited until he'd gone before she turned to Jody. "So, what's his story?"

Chapter Fourteen

Jody

She was unable to tell Daphne everything to start with. They had to wait for Aoife to arrive, along with emergency services, who took Bob Smith to the hospital. He had woken shortly before the EMTs arrived, and he looked stricken and horrified. From her brief interaction with him, the real him, he'd seemed to be a polite and quiet man, and she felt sorry for the burden he would have to carry with the memory of Honsiu's invasion.

She planned to talk to him before he left the hospital in Harrow Bay, though she imagined he'd forget everything within a few weeks. She couldn't help wondering if the magic was strong enough to completely sublimate the memory of what had happened to him. She suspected he might have vague nightmares for years, and it seemed unfair for him not to know the source, but maybe it was better if he didn't have to relive or remember the demonic invasion of his body.

They headed home after the station was empty, though there was no sign of Beez yet. Jody figured he must be out doing something to entertain himself, and she briefly wondered if he had a girlfriend of some sort around Harrow Bay. She decided she didn't want to speculate about that, so she shut down the line of inquiry before her mind could fully develop it.

In the SUV on the way back to her house, Daphne asked again, "What is Drake? He doesn't seem like he's a vampire."

"He's half-demon. Before you freak out, he wasn't made a demon, and he wasn't created from his own evil actions. His father was a demon who seduced his human mother. His boss saved him."

Daphne's eyebrow slowly arched toward her hairline. "His boss?"

"Two guesses as to who that might be, and I'm sure you'll only need one."

Daphne's eyes widened. "You said there's a Hell gate in the middle of town? Does that mean this town is owned by Hell or something?"

"No, not at all. I suspect the Hell gate's here for the same reason the town is. There are a series of ley lines, which are pathways power can move through the Earth, and a strong nexus point where the Hell gate is. Likely, the ley lines drew the people who started Harrow Bay, though I couldn't tell you which came first—the town or the Hell gate. Probably the Hell gate, but it might've been just a small inconvenience to the pioneers of the town."

"Fascinating." Daphne didn't seem sarcastic. "Why didn't you tell me all this?"

"Part of my job is keeping the secret, and once you leave, you'll forget all about it within a few weeks." She shrugged. "It didn't seem like anything I'd have to mention to you, at least until you met Ryland. Then I struggled with how much I should say and when."

"I wish you'd said something sooner. I can handle the truth, you know?"

Jody bit her tongue, deciding not to point out how well Daphne had reacted to the news when she'd told her earlier. It must've taken a demonstration from Ryland for her to believe he was a vampire. "I was trying to balance your safety and my job. It's a crappy situation to be in, to be honest."

"I'm really sorry I didn't listen when you tried to warn me in more subtle ways. Then I rushed into being converted by Ryland..." She trailed off, and Jody realized why as she pulled into the driveway. Ryland stood on her front porch.

She looked at Daphne. "Do you want me to get rid of him?"

Daphne hesitated for a moment, and then she shook her head. "No, we need to talk. I rushed out of there, and I'm sure he's just worried about me."

"Why don't you talk in the house? I'm not going to eavesdrop, but I'm there if you need me."

Daphne smiled at her, but she seemed a lot calmer than she had before. "I think it'll be okay if we talk outside. You know how loudly I can shout if I need to."

Jody smiled in agreement, though she wished her friend would reconsider. She wondered then if vampires really had the ability to compel someone to do something, but she couldn't envision it working on Daphne even if he were the world's strongest vampire.

That didn't mean she didn't lurk near the door when she went inside. Gram and her mother were on the sofa, and she put up her finger to her lips, wanting silence. She couldn't hear what they were discussing, or at least not the words themselves. The tone remained reasonably congenial, and she never heard any loud shouts, or even anything that sounded like a sharp, angry note.

When she heard Daphne's high-heeled boots on the porch, she rushed from the door and quickly took a seat in the chair, hoping Daphne wouldn't know she'd been lurking so close.

Her friend shot her a knowing look as she came inside. "How much did you hear?" she asked with a smile as she sat down on the last cushion on the couch, placing her beside Isabel.

"I didn't hear anything. Just tones. Everything sounded okay. Is it?"

After a moment, Daphne nodded. "I think so. We both decided we were rushing into things, and I'm embarrassed to admit it, but I think part of the reason I asked him to change me into a vampire—"

"You did what?" asked Willa with a gasp. "Are you crazy, Daphne?"

"It's okay, Willa. I changed my mind." Apparently, Daphne decided to spare her mother the account of just when she'd changed her mind, or what had happened before and after. "Anyway, we decided to slow things down. When he told me the first thing he noticed about me was how much I look like Nila, his old girlfriend, I admit that gave me some pause."

"He told me that you look like her, but you're nothing like her, and he likes you just as you are."

Daphne arched a brow. "Are you actually defending him to me, Jody? My, you've changed." She laughed, and it was a tinkling sound of delight. "I don't think he's into me just because I look like some girl he was in a relationship with eighty years ago. There's definitely a connection between us, but it makes sense to take time and figure out what kind of connection. We need to know if it's something that can last for a year, or even a decade, before we rush into something that could join us for centuries."

"Do vampires age?" asked Isabel, pointedly ignoring Willa's choking sound of protest at the question.

"Slightly and slowly. I wouldn't live forever, but I would live for a very long time. I want to make sure I'm ready for that step with Ryland before I take it."

Jody looked at her mom, who still looked slightly aghast, but she didn't seem like she planned to hurl herself into the river of denial and pretend this hadn't occurred. She gave her a sympathetic glance before looking at Daphne again. "Does that mean you're staying around Harrow Bay for a while?"

Daphne sighed. "I can't right now. I have some travel plans. I'll be back in a few weeks though, at least for a few days. I want to return often enough that I don't forget what's going on here, what Ryland is, or everything about Harrow Bay." Daphne let out a small sigh. "From what I've seen, I could see being happy here, minus the crazy demon lizard things. Does that happen a lot?"

"Practically never," said Jody with a grin.

At the same time, Willa frowned sharply. "What demon lizard things?"

Jody leaned over and patted her on the knee. "Don't worry, Mom. I'll tell you later." But only if Willa actually asked again and didn't convince herself this was something to ignore.

***

Jody had gone to bed and been there for a while, having fallen asleep, before her phone chimed. She picked it up and swiped it to open, finding a text message from Drake to let her know he was downstairs. She climbed out of bed, careful not to disturb Daphne, and slid on a robe. She padded downstairs and opened the back door for him, letting him in and steering him toward the kitchen table. "It's quieter here, and we won't wake the others."

He nodded as he sat down. He looked weary.

"Are you all right? Are you hungry?"

His stomach rumbled in response. "I'm starving. By the time we sat through the trial and the punishment, I could've eaten one of the lesser demons raw if I had some ketchup." He gave her a half-grin, but it didn't quite reach his eyes.

Jody stood up and went to the fridge, quickly grabbing ingredients for a sandwich that she assembled for him. "What trial?"

"Honsiu's trial. It's a bit of a kangaroo court, honestly. If you're summoned before Luc's tribunal, you're pretty much presumed guilty already. He practically knows everything, you know?"

She nodded, for she imagined it would be that way. "So, you had time for a trial?"

"And punishment." He grimaced in distaste. "Honsiu was an evil piece of work, but..." he trailed off. "Never mind."

It was obvious he didn't want to talk about it, and she didn't really want to hear about Honsiu's fate, other than assuring herself he was gone. "He won't be back?"

"I don't see how." Drake took the sandwich she offered, cramming the layers down so he could stuff half of it in his mouth in one bite. "Sorry," he said around a mouthful. "Starving."

She waved a hand, not overly concerned with his lack of manners right then. "Do you get something special for bringing him in?"

Drake shrugged. "The continued ability to move freely between the realms, I suppose. I have that privilege as long as I'm useful to him."

"Is there some way out of it?" She reached over and touched his free hand as she asked.

He shook his head. "Unless you know how to extract my demon DNA?"

"Sadly not." It was one of the realities of dating Drake. She had to live with the fact that he worked as a bounty hunter for Hell, and he reported to Lucifer. That was the truth of the situation, and it was a huge stumbling block, but it certainly wasn't big enough to keep her from wanting to be with him.

"How's Daphne?"

"Just a little shaken up, but she took the truth well, and I don't think she lost enough blood to be worried about." At his surprised look, she quickly explained how Daphne had started to undergo the transformation before changing her mind abruptly.

"Her blood must have been what coaxed Honsiu out of the storeroom and put him in attack-mode."

She nodded, having reached the same conclusion. "I think the homeless man he attacked might have been bleeding too. He asked the pharmacist for Neosporin for a bad cut on his leg."

"Honsiu is a blood demon, and he'd find fresh blood practically irresistible, especially since he was weakened by his escape from Hell." He finished the last section of his sandwich. "I'm glad she's okay, and they're slowing down. How are you?"

"Still a little freaked out by that thing I saw, but I'm okay. I can move my mouth and my face again, and I feel much better knowing he's back in Hell where he belongs." She lowered her voice. "And you're back with me, where you belong."

His eyes widened. "With you?"

She shrugged. "Yeah, I was thinking about it earlier, after Daphne fell asleep, but before I did. We've been taking it slowly, and I'm not suggesting we rush into anything, but I think we should consider becoming intimate again." She put up a hand. "Not now, of course. Daphne's asleep in my bed."

He laughed, sounding relieved. "I'm happy to hear that, honestly, because I'm beat. I can't impress you with my prowess and stamina tonight. I'm going to have to ride Evita home, and that's hard enough."

Jody shook her head. "You should just sleep on the couch."

He groaned. "That might be almost as bad as riding out to my cabin, but I'm tired enough that I think I will."

Jody stayed with him while he polished off an apple for dessert before walking with him into the living room. He stretched out on the couch, then spent the next few minutes talking with her as she curled up in the chair nearby, brushing her fingers through his hair and caressing his forehead lightly until he started to snore.

She could go up to bed then, but she found she didn't want to just yet. Sitting in the serenity around her, filled only with his soft snores of exhaustion, was the most peaceful place she could think of, and she had no desire to end the moment, even though Drake slept on. She continued to stroke his hair until her hand grew tired, but even then, she kept it on his head and maintained a real and solid connection between them.

******

The Harrow Bay adventure continues in "Mermaids & Mood Swings[1]."

---

1. https://www.amazon.com/gp/product/B08Y7Y5SQD

About Aurelia

Aurelia Skye is the pen name *USA Today* bestselling author Kit Tunstall uses when writing science fiction romance. It's simply a way to separate the myriad types of stories she writes so readers know what to expect with each "author."

If you enjoyed this story and would like to receive notifications of new releases or access bonus chapters for your favorite books, please join my Mailing List[1]**. You'll also receive free books just for joining. If you prefer to receive notifications for just one, or a few, of my pen names, you'll have the option to select which lists to subscribe to at signup.**

---

1. http://kittunstall.com/newsletter/

Did you love *Mermaids & Mood Swings*? Then you should read *Vampires & Varicose Veins*[2] by Aurelia Skye!

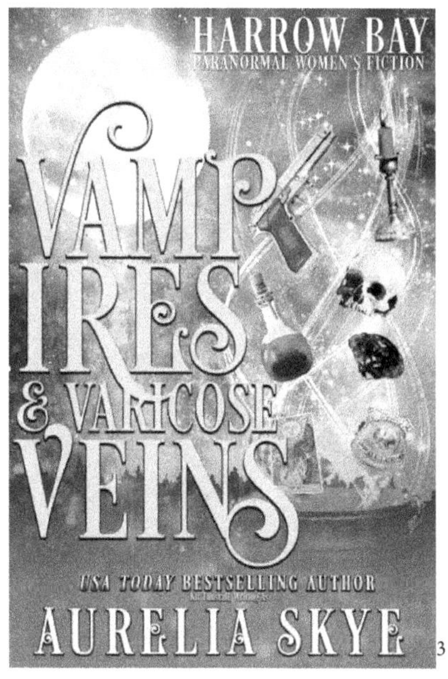

BFFs and Bloodsuckers Shouldn't Mix When Jody's BFF blows through town, she has to shield Daphne from the truth of Harrow Bay. Her friend complicates that when she starts dating Ryland. Jody is nervous about her being with a vampire, especially when Daphne doesn't know what he is. With Drake busy chasing an extremely dangerous, high-level escapee from Hell, and having to contend with the temporary deputy sent to fill in for Michael while he's on vacation, Jody feels stretched thin.Willa and Patty traverse new ground, and Isabel makes a new friend. Things are much the same, but everything is different and constantly in flux. In other words, it's a normal day in Harrow Bay...as normal as things ever are. Jody just has to keep it

---

2. https://books2read.com/u/3n2JN8

3. https://books2read.com/u/3n2JN8

all together, hide the secret of the town, and potentially protect her friend from a suitor who might want to give more than love bites. No problem. Right?

Also by Aurelia Skye

Celestial Mates
Wrong Place, Right Mate
Destined For The Drakari Warlords

Cybernetic Hearts
Mated To The Cyborg General
Claimed By The Cyborg Commander
Fated For The Cyborg Officer
Meant For The Cyborg Captain
Baby For The Cyborg General
Cybernetic Hearts: Complete Series

Dazon Agenda
Written In The Stars
Alien's Babies
Diplomatic Affairs
Moon Madness
Across The Stars
Emperor's Assassin Bride
Dazon Agenda: Complete Collection

Future Fairytales
Hooked

Harrow Bay
Hell Gates & Hot Flashes
Nightmares & Night Sweats
Warlocks & Wrinkles
Love Spells & Liver Spots
Phantasms & Presbyopia
Vampires & Varicose Veins
Mermaids & Mood Swings
Séances & Sagging Skin
Necromancy & Knee Pains
Marids & Memory Loss
Devil Deals & Dizzy Spells

Hell Virus
Catching Hell
Surviving Hell
Bleeding Hell
Raising Hell
Sharing Hell

Howls Romance
The Jaguar Alpha's Forbidden Lover

Olympus Station
Station Commander's Surrogate
Alien Prince's Secret Baby
Security Agent's Alien Bartender
Olympus Station Compilation

SpicyShorts
Music In My Heart
Kilted Tentacle Monster: A Search for True Love

True North
True North #1: Death & Deception
True North #2: Rescued & Revelations
True North #3: Fire & Ice
True North #4: Enemies & Lovers
True North #5: Truth & Tiranog
True North #6: Fight & Flight
True North #7: Love & Loss

Wounded Warriors
Relentless
Marked
Justice
Wounded Warriors Collection
Hunted